THE
Forever
GAME

Katy ♡ xoxo
Archer

KATY ARCHER

THE FOREVER GAME
Nolan U Hockey #6

Cover Design © Designed with Grace

ISBN: 978-1-991138-30-9 (ebook)
ISBN: 978-1-991138-32-3 (paperback)

Archer Street Romance
www.katyarcher.com

CHAPTER 1
BAXTER

I'm getting married tomorrow.

Finally. This wedding has been three years in the making, and I'm so ready for it. I'm more than ready. It should have happened years ago, but one thing after another has thwarted our plans.

But not this time.

Tomorrow afternoon, I'll be waiting at the end of the aisle to watch my stunning bride walk toward me. It's going to be epic.

We just need to get through the rehearsal dinner first.

So not my thing, but it's tradition, right?

I shake the hand of Tammy's uncle. I should remember the guy's name, but I don't see the Tan family much. Once a year at Christmas is hardly enough, and I'm already flustered tonight.

For one, I'm in a suit and tie, which feels more like a straitjacket and noose around my neck. Tammy is on the other side of the room, greeting guests with her perfect smile and bubbly nature. In these situations, I feel kind of lost when she's not by my side. Kai's got his arm around her waist and is clinging pretty close. I get it. I wish I could do the same... and start working my way across the room as soon as I'm able.

"How's it going, man?"

I grin at Casey, giving him a look that says it all.

He laughs and slaps me on the shoulder. "It'll all be over soon, bro. Don't worry about it."

I notice his loosened tie and disheveled hair and feel a surge of envy. Wish I could do the same. Wish I could lose the tie altogether and be in jeans and my comfy work boots.

"I just have to survive tonight and the ceremony. Then I can relax."

"Yeah, well, at least the rehearsal's done so we all know where to stand and shit." Casey laughs.

I nod, then glance down at Caroline, who's sitting at the table with a small frown.

She's pregnant and looks ready to pop. The baby isn't due for a month yet, but she's been complaining about the heat and muttering, "How am I going to last another four weeks!"

I heard her say that to Lani before as she wiped her brow with a napkin and shifted in her chair, rubbing her lower back and mumbling about feeling like a whale.

Casey follows my line of sight, brushing his hand over his wife's shoulder, then playing with the ends of her hair while she continues talking to Lani, who has a loved-up smile on her face. Maybe being at this wedding is finally getting her in the mood to marry Asher. They've been dating for so long with not even a hint of a proposal in sight. Tomorrow, she's a bridesmaid and he's a groomsman. Maybe standing up front during our practice run got them thinking about their own future.

According to the rumor mill that seems to run continually no matter how far apart we all live, Asher really wants to propose, but Lani has told it to him straight that she's not ready until after she's finished her doctorate. Who knows how long that will take? She's been studying for forever!

It's driving Asher a little insane... and last I heard, he was planning on just ignoring her request and popping the question. I don't know if he's done it yet, though.

Lani laughs at something Caroline just said, giving her wrist a sympathetic squeeze while Asher grins between them, kissing Lani's bare shoulder before skimming his fingers down her arm.

"Sorry I'm late." I spin and smile at a flustered-looking Liam. It's unusual to see him out of sorts like this. He's usually cool and calm, but there's a marked frown on his face that he's struggling to hide.

I shake his hand. "No worries, man. Rachel warned us that you were tied up at work. Glad you could make it."

"Thanks." He nods and starts scanning the room for his wife. As soon as he spots her, he seems to relax and looks back at me, his lips curling up at the edges. "The rehearsal go okay?"

"Yep." I grin. "Rachel is the perfect maid of honor. Tammy's in good hands."

Liam's smile grows a little wider. "She was so touched when Tammy asked all those years ago. I'm stoked it's finally happening for real."

"Tell me about it." I bulge my eyes, then let out a throaty chuckle. It's edged with a nervousness I can't hide. There's less than twenty-four hours to go until Tammy's officially my wife, and if history has taught me anything... that's still plenty of time for things to completely bomb.

Casey moves around me, slapping Liam on the shoulder. "You good, dude?"

He gives an awkward nod before sighing. "Just a tough day. Shift ran over, and I hate being late." The tense set of his jaw tells me the lateness is probably the smallest factor. I wonder what he saw on the streets today. He doesn't tell too many cop stories—he's a stickler for protocol and respecting the rights of the people he arrests—but we can always tell when he's had a harrowing day. Not sure what went down, but it can't have been pretty. I'm sure the constant stream of rain didn't help either.

I smile again, wanting to ease his tension. Man, I'm desperate to ask for deets, but he won't spill, and I actually admire him more for the fact that he's not a big gossip.

Nolan might be a small town, but there's still some pretty heinous shit that goes on behind the scenes, and Liam has to face it all.

"Well, time to put that shit behind you and enjoy the night." Casey grins, and I step aside so he can take a seat at the Hockey House table.

Rachel glides up to Liam's side, lightly kissing his lips and cupping his cheek. She murmurs something that I can't hear, and he gives her a tired, sad smile before kissing her again. For some reason, I keep watching them for a moment longer. They've had to deal with some tough shit this year, and—

Rachel's eyes dart across the table, her lips jerking into a tense smile that is so un-Rachel-like, my eyebrows jump up in surprise.

"Hey, Liam," Caroline murmurs softly, her smile just as tight as Rachel's.

"Hi, Caroline." His voice is rumbly and deep, like he's walking through a minefield just saying hello to her, and my gut twists as both girls turn away and Liam winces, rubbing his forehead.

I frown at Casey. His eyes throw me a clear "don't ask" warning, his brow wrinkling as he looks at the back of Rachel's head. I don't know what's going on, but it can't be good. Rachel is the sweetest human being on the planet, and the girls are usually so tight with each other. This frosty reception is so not good for happy rehearsal dinner vibes... and Ethan and Mikayla aren't really helping either.

The bright smile that usually lights Mick's face is nowhere to be seen. I'm pretty good at observing people, and I can tell, even from across the table, that she's not having a great day.

Ethan's watching her, lightly running his hand down her back, but he's not looking happy either.

Actually, when I think about it, they both came in kind of tense and snippy. Maybe they got into a fight on the way here.

This is just great. Tammy's special night is going to be ruined by these douchebags if they don't shake off whatever they all walked in with.

I want to snap at them to get their shit together, but I'm interrupted by Kai.

"Hey, Dad." He jumps behind me, wrapping his skinny arms around my waist.

I spin to hug him back. "Hey, buddy."

"Mom says it's time to take a seat and get started with speeches and stuff."

"Sounds good." I squeeze his shoulder and wink down at him. "Go tell Mom I'll be there in just a sec."

"'Kay." He bounds off, his gangly nine-year-old legs taking him across the room at speed.

He started calling me Dad after his little sister was born. Nova's just turned two, so she's still learning to speak, but Kai was determined that Mama, Dada, and Kai would be her first three words, so he's been pushing hard for that outcome. It worked out well for me, because hearing him call me Dad is one of the best things in the world. I love that kid like he's my own.

Nova's not here tonight. My dad took her home after the rehearsal and volunteered to skip the dinner so he could watch her. He knows as well as the rest of us that my daughter is dynamite, and she would not cope well with this situation. She'd have a blast, but it'd be like trying to tame a tornado, and Tammy and I wouldn't get more than halfway through a sentence before having to chase after her. And when she gets around Casey and Caroline's boys, it's a full-blown hurricane. Thankfully, neither of them are here tonight either.

Tammy wanted a fancy, formal dinner, which means no toddlers are around to terrorize the guests.

I grin, thinking about my beautiful girl and wondering if Dad has managed to get her down for the night. That girl has my old man wrapped around her little finger. They adore each other, and he's probably feeding her popsicles and letting her watch an entire Barbie movie. She'll fall asleep on his lap, and he'll be the happiest guy on the planet.

Tomorrow should be interesting. Who knows what havoc she'll get up to as the flower girl. Kai's determined to keep her in check, but it's a big ask for the kid. Thankfully, Nova thinks her big brother hung the moon and will usually do what he tells her... for all of two minutes.

I'm chuckling by the time I reach the table. Tammy smiles at me, and I lightly kiss her lips as I sit down.

"You good?" she murmurs against my mouth.

"Yeah, you know how much I love these kinds of things." I say it in a bright voice, which only makes her giggle.

"I know, right? I had such high hopes, but then I get here and am like... why are we doing this again?"

"What do you mean?" I lean toward her, cupping her elbow and checking her face for signs of distress. "Is everything okay?"

"Yeah." She nods, but I don't believe her.

My eyebrows pull together and she relents with a sigh. "My parents are... being my parents." She shrugs.

I let out an irritated huff, wondering what they've said to make her feel bad this time.

Glancing down the table, I check that they're behaving themselves. Thankfully, they're talking to Uncle What-His-Name and looking nonthreatening... for now.

"You giving a speech, son?" Grandpa takes a seat beside me.

"Yeah." I pull out my index cards, my hands starting to shake.

Stupid traditions. Why the hell do we do this stuff?

You're doing it for Tammy. Just focus on her and you'll get through this.

I glance up and notice she's watching me. Her pained smile hurts my chest, and I lightly brush my fingers down her face and whisper, "I love you. I'd do anything for you."

"I know giving speeches is not your thing. I'm so—"

"Don't apologize," I quickly cut her off before she can. "I love you, TT."

Her smile is beautiful, and I rise from my seat before I can chicken out.

Asher notices and starts tapping his fork against his wine glass.

"Speech!" Casey pumps his fist in the air. "Go, Bax-Man!"

I cringe as a cheer goes up from the Hockey House table. Tamara's mom looks like she's been sucking on a lemon as she gives the unruly bunch a disapproving glare.

Clearing my throat, I focus back on my bride-to-be. She takes my hand, her brown gaze bright with affection.

"I, uh..." I clear my throat again and check my cards before scanning the tables around me. "Thank you all for coming. Tammy and I are so happy you could make it."

"Finally!" Ethan calls out, and everyone starts to laugh.

"True. Looks like we're actually going to make it this time." I grin. "Thanks for sticking with us. I love this beautiful woman beside me so much." I glance down at her, then wink at Kai. "My family is the most important thing to me, and being able to make it all official tomorrow is something I've wanted for a long time now."

Tammy grins up at me and mouths, "I love you."

"We—"

Someone's phone starts ringing, and I pause, fighting a smile when I see Mikayla jerk in her seat, her eyes bulging in apology as she wrestles out her device, then winces and gets up from the table, running out of the room to answer the call.

Ethan watches her go—a dark, irritated grimace scrunching his face.

I'm not sure what that's about, but I'm once again struck by the unsettling vibes that seem to be emanating from so many of my friends tonight. Everything just seems kind of off, and that was not what I was hoping for coming into my wedding. It's like Tammy and I are cursed when it comes to this big day.

This is attempt number three, and I have to make this work for her.

"So, yeah... uh... just wanted to say a big thank you to all my friends and family who are here celebrating with us. And I want to honor my gorgeous woman who I've loved since I was ten years old."

Tammy squeezes my hand.

"I can't wait to finally marry you tomorrow. Being your husband has been a long-time goal for me, and I'll be the best one I possibly can be."

"You're going to be amazing." Tammy jumps up, wrapping her arms around my neck and pulling me down for a kiss.

Our guests start cheering and applauding for us.

We pull away from each other, Tammy giggling, and I brush the tip of my nose against hers before smiling out across the room. My mouth dips as Ethan jerks out of his seat with an angry frown and stalks out of the room after his wife.

Concern washes through me and is only amplified when Caroline starts wincing and rubbing her forehead. She's obviously uncomfortable and wants to leave too.

I catch Casey's eye and tip my head for the door, letting him know he can go. He looks disappointed, standing with a glum smile and helping Caroline up. She cradles her belly, walking out of the room with barely a goodbye.

Rachel watches her go, tears lining her lashes.

Liam leans in to comfort her, and I get that sick feeling in the pit of my stomach again.

I'm getting married tomorrow, and the people who are most important to me seem to be a fractured mess.

I want this wedding to be perfect for Tammy, but I can't shake the feeling that we're heading into yet another disaster.

Seven months ago, Tammy asked something of me, and I swore I'd make it happen for her.

Shit, what if I can't keep my promise?

SEVEN MONTHS EARLIER...

NOVEMBER

CHAPTER 2
TAMMY

Nova is being extra fussy tonight. I rock her back and forth, humming her a tune as I try to get my overactive toddler to sleep. She's eighteen months old now, and from the second she was born, I could tell she was the complete opposite of Kai. He was always so quiet and cuddly. He took his time to study people and decide if they were worthy of a smile. He'd watch and observe before acting. My little Supernova, on the other hand, is a ball of energy. She started smiling at only four weeks, which apparently is very young. She'll babble at anyone she meets, and she didn't learn to walk, she learned to *run*. From the second she wakes until the moment she crashes, she's on the go, and it's exhausting... and entertaining. She has definitely filled our house with sunshine. And fireworks. And rainstorms. And tornados.

"Come on, baby. It's okay," I murmur against her cheek. "Let yourself go and fall asleep."

She whimpers and rubs her nose across my shirt. I cradle the back of her head and finish humming "Blackbird" by the Beatles. I don't know why I picked that song and made it ours, but it just came to me one night, and it's stuck. Beyonce did a beautiful version of the song, and it's become a favorite of mine.

By the time I get to the end, Nova has gone limp in my arms.

Finally!

I don't usually rock her to sleep, but on those days when she's been hyper, she gets herself into this vortex of overactivity, and it makes it so hard for her to fall asleep. I creep to her crib and lay her down, lightly stroking her head before covering her with blankets and making sure Mr. Pickles is within easy reach.

I leave the door ajar in case she wakes in the night, then check on Kai, who's starfishing in his bed, his limbs looking long and gangly. Puberty is only a year or so away for the little guy, but I can already see his body getting longer. He's stretching out like a piece of gum, and I swear he's going to be taller than me by the time he's a teenager. Watching him grow and develop warms my heart to no end. He's the sweetest boy and the most patient big brother. Nova adores him, and he'll chase her around, trying to protect her from her wild antics all the livelong day. School is a nice reprieve for him, and he's made a best friend—Tommy—who is the sweetest kid. I'm just so happy for my boy that he's got a little buddy.

Just like I had with Baxter.

I grin, walking to the master bedroom and thinking how my little buddy became so much more. From the way Kai blushed at the girls at the fall dance this year, I don't think Tommy and Kai's relationship is going to shift the way Baxter's and mine did.

My smile grows a little wider as I walk into my room and spot Baxter on our bed. He's shirtless, and I admire his hard ridges. His handyman business keeps him strong and toned. He's seriously the sexiest man on the planet, and when he sits on our bed, writing in his journal with that intent look on his face, my heart falls a little more in love with him.

I wonder what he's writing but try not to ask too often. It's his personal space to get out his thoughts and feelings. He lets me read it when I ask, but I try to respect his privacy.

Squirting some hand cream into my palm, I rub the moisturizer into my skin and watch my man. He really is the most beautiful sight—his long legs stretched out on the bed, those beautiful bare feet, those solid muscles I want to run my hands over. And his face, so sweet and kind and—

"What?" He doesn't look up from his journal, and I grin, loving the way he can sense my perusal.

"I want you to be my husband."

He glances up and starts to laugh. "Not sure that's ever gonna happen, TT."

"But it must." I slip off his big hoodie, letting it drop to the floor before I crawl across the bed and kneel beside him. "I want to make you mine."

"I am yours." He lays his journal aside, cinching me around the waist and lifting me onto his lap. I straddle his legs, loving the way his fingers draw lines up my thighs, creeping beneath his extra-large T-shirt and settling around my curvy ass. I'm not toned and sculpted like him. My curves are soft and squishy, but he always makes me feel so sexy.

His eyes gleam with a heat that makes my body tremble, but I try to stay on point and finish our conversation.

Cupping his face, I brush my thumb across his perfect lips and smile. "I want to make it official."

"Okay." He tips his head back to think. "So, we got engaged three years ago and have planned the wedding twice…"

I wince. "Third time's the charm?"

"You sure you want to try again?" His face crumples to match mine. "We could just go to the courthouse."

"No." I shake my head, stubbornly adamant about this. "I want a proper wedding. We had so many great ideas, and I want them to happen. Nova's old enough now." He gives me a skeptical frown, and I can't help giggling. "There will be plenty of people there to keep an eye on her. Plenty of hands to grab her before she can destroy anything."

He laughs along with me and shakes his head, an adoring smile creeping over his face. She is most definitely a daddy's girl. Their bond is adorable. The way he is with her makes my heart melt every time; it's basically become a permanent blob of putty in my chest.

I need this man to be my husband. I mean, he basically is, but there's just something about making it all official that appeals to me so damn much. I want to be able to refer to him as my husband.

"We have to make this happen." I kiss his lips, then spring back, trying to sell this some more. "The chances of you getting the flu again the day before our wedding have got to be slim to none, right? I mean, that would just be a freak of nature."

He smiles up at me, giving my butt a little squeeze. "You'll be able to fit into your dress again now."

"Yes, I will." I resist the urge to tell him it'll be a tight squeeze, but I will be fitting into my wedding dress, dammit. And Baxter's flu and my puke-filled pregnancy are not going to stop us this time. "It's not like we're starting from scratch. Let's just do it."

"When?"

"This summer, the way we originally planned. My coursework will be done for the year, and I've been saving up my vacation time at the center. I'll take a few weeks off so we can honeymoon right after."

His eyes glow at the mention of a honeymoon. I'm sure between our parents we could easily find care for the kids, so Baxter and I could get some alone time.

"Plus, my summer wedding dress will be perfect for the event." I think about that stunning dress, specially designed for me, and feel a trill of excitement.

Baxter grabs his phone and checks the calendar app. "That's seven months away."

"I know, plenty of time to book and plan."

"We won't be able to get the same venue."

"That's okay. We'll find something else. There's bound to be something around." I give him a hopeful smile. "I swear, nothing can stop it this time." My eyes start to glint as I lean against him, our lips less than an inch apart. "I am going to will this wedding into existence. I am going to make you my husband, Baxter Brown."

He presses his smile against mine, his tongue darting into my mouth and swiping mine before he pulls back and whispers, "I'm going to make it happen for you, TT. I promise."

And I know he means it.

Yes! We're getting married!

After all this time and all these setbacks, it's finally going to happen.

"I love you," I murmur, not even giving him a chance to reply before kissing his lips, his chin, his neck, and licking my way down his perfect torso.

He groans, rasping, "Are the kids asleep?"

"Uh-huh." I curl my fingers into the waistband of his boxers, and he helps me yank them off. His cock—so hard and eager for me—springs out to greet me, and I smile, licking the tip as he grips my shirt and starts to pull it off.

We play a game of Tammy Says. It's my favorite game

in the world—a special one for just me and my best friend.

"Tammy says... let me suck this gorgeous cock."

Baxter cups the back of my head as I go down on him, heating us both up for what comes next. I work him until he's groaning, his legs squirming, on the cusp of an orgasm, before pulling away. I don't want it to be over yet. Sitting up, I crawl back toward him. I'm usually full of way more instructions than this, ordering him around on this bed, but tonight, all I can rasp is "Tammy says... make love to your future wife."

He grins as I perch myself over his tip, my wet folds weeping with anticipation. Grabbing my hips, he pulls me down onto him, and I let out a soft cry as he fills me all the way to my soul.

He's the best thing that ever happened to me.

I want to tell him that, but words are impossible right now. Gazing into his gorgeous eyes, I try to tell him as we ride this erotic train together—our breaths mingling, our hands gliding, our fingers pinching, our chests heaving until he's making me come with whimpers and groans and following right after, crying my name while squeezing my ass and pumping into me. I sink onto him, grinding my hips until I've taken as much of him as I can handle, cherishing this blissful moment.

He wraps his arms around me, kissing my shoulder while he catches his breath. I close my eyes, resting my chin against his neck and whispering over and over, "I love you, Baxter Brown. And I can't wait to be your wife."

CHAPTER 3
CASEY

"Are you serious?" I laugh, gripping the wheel and navigating my way home as I talk to Baxter. It's been a hectic week of travel and away games, and I can't wait to bust in the door and hug my family again. When I first went pro, Caroline would join me for any games she could, but since having kids, it's just too hard.

I didn't mean to get her pregnant her senior year of college. Thankfully, she was able to still pass everything and graduate before Billy was born. But then Troy came along before she had a chance to get back to work, so she decided to stay home and just focus on the kids for a few years. I know she's looking forward to joining the workforce again soon but wants to wait until Troy is at least two before starting him in daycare. He'll just do half days the way Billy's been doing and then build up from there. She's got it all mapped out, and I just go with the flow.

She's been doing a little part-time work from home—data entry and statical analysis for a small company in Denver—which is enough to keep her brain engaged, but it's not a long-term solution.

"Yes, I am," Baxter assures me. "No matter what, this wedding is going to happen. I promised Tammy, and I have to keep it, man."

"I'm sure you will. There's no way you'd have to cancel the wedding a third time."

"Let's hope so," Baxter grumbles, and I can't help laughing again.

"Whatever you need, bro. I'm here for you."

"Yeah, I know. Thanks. Can you just make sure you keep June 28 free on your calendar?"

"I'll lock it in as soon as I get home. You guys tying the knot in Nolan?"

"Yep. Not sure of exact venue yet, but we're working on it. The church is available, but we're still looking for the best place to have the reception. I'll keep you posted."

"Sounds good. Can I bring the whole tribe, or is this an adults-only thing?"

"Well, my kids will be there, obviously, but..." He hesitates, and I can't help snickering.

"My boys and your little Supernova together are explosive. I get it. Maybe I'll just get Caroline's parents to come up to Nolan with us."

"Good call." Baxter sounds more than grateful, and I get it.

Thank God for my in-laws. They have been a total

godsend. Not only did her father marry us the summer after she graduated—about a month before Billy was born—but when Caroline and Billy first shifted to Centennial, Caroline's parents joined us before the hockey season began. They relocated their lives to be close to their daughter and support her. Caroline visits them at least twice a week, and our boys adore their Gramps and Granny.

Being away so much during the season makes things hard. Caroline's a great mom, but she gets a little stressed out sometimes, and she's basically given up a career to stay at home with the kids. That was her choice, and she's glad she's doing it, but some days get the better of her. Raising kids is hard work. Especially two rambunctious boys. She often talks about wanting a sweet, sedate girl, but then the idea of having a third kid freaks her out. I haven't said it—because I value my life—but I'm sure we'll have more. I love being a dad so damn much and want a whole bunch of kids. When Caroline's ready. Hopefully I can convince her.

A grin grows on my face as I picture my sexy-ass wife. God, I can't wait to bury my fingers in her red curls and kiss those luscious lips of hers. As soon as the kids are down for the night, she's mine. I am going to enjoy every inch of her body. Shit, even thinking about holding her and tasting her delicious tits is making my dick twitch. A week without my woman is too long. As much as I adore hockey, I can't wait for the season to be over so I can spend more time with her.

I walk in the door and don't even have a chance to put my stuff on the ground before Billy is barreling into me.

"Daddy!" he screams, launching himself at my chest. I catch him with a laugh, making fart noises on his neck while he giggles and squirms in my arms. He's the most fun-loving three-year-old with his blond curls and big blue eyes. He's got energy to burn, and I love his enthusiasm for everything.

Fezzik trots into the room, his tail wagging as he barks me a greeting, then rests his little paws on my leg. I pat his head, then glance up to see the sweetest boy in the world toddling toward me.

"Da-da-da-da." Troy raises his little arms for a cuddle as he stamps his excited feet on the ground and nearly topples over. I catch his arm, hauling him up against me and hugging both my boys.

I love these guys too much. Seriously. My heart is close to bursting as I tickle their waists and they squirm and scream. With a roar, I lumber into the living room and drop to the floor, commencing our standard wrestling match as the boys jump all over me, giggling and dribbling on my shirt as I throw them around, catching them before they hit the floor and hurt themselves. They roll and jump back to their feet, launching themselves on me again while I try to figure out the best way to wrap this up. As adorable as their hysterical laughter is—seriously, I can't get enough of that sound—it's time to put an end to this before one of them accidentally pukes on me.

Besides, I want to find Caroline and hug her, feel her curves pressed against me while I breathe in her beautiful scent and—

A flash of red appears in the archway and I glance up, grinning at my woman—who's glaring at me like I'm the world's worst human... *uh, what the fuck?*—before getting torpedoed by Billy.

"Omph!" I start coughing, trying to catch my breath as sharp little elbows and knees dig into all the wrong places. "Time out! Time out!" I call above their giggles and shouts. The boys eventually hear me and start to settle down. Wrapping my arms around them both, I give them a careful look and whisper, "Is Mommy okay?"

Billy's lip sticks out and he shrugs while Troy just gives me a big smile, drool dripping off his bottom lip. I catch it with my finger and wipe it on my shirt, laughing at his dopey expression. I rise from the floor, a boy on each hip, and wander down the hallway.

By the time I reach the kitchen, cupboard doors are slamming and Caroline is slapping a chopping board onto the counter with a growl. I would seriously hate to be that cucumber right now, because that thing is going to get sliced and diced with fucking fury.

I study her from the edge of the room before inching toward the highchairs. "Hey, Cherry Girl."

"Welcome home," she mutters, refusing to look at me.

I slide Billy into his chair, then strap Troy into his, pulling the tray close so he can't wriggle free. Caroline has already prepared their afternoon snack, and I start dropping blueberries and Cheerios onto their trays. I also give Billy some apple slices. Two sippy cups later and I'm hands-free to hug my wife. I step up behind her frenzied salad making and go to wrap my arms around her.

"Oh no you don't." She nudges me off.

"What?" I step back with a surprised laugh.

"You are not touching me right now, Casey Pierce."

My forehead crinkles. "Why? What'd I do?"

"Every time your horny ass gets home, I can't resist you, and then this happens!" Her hands flick up in time with her pitching voice, and I duck to avoid getting stabbed in the eye as she pushes me aside to throw away the food scraps.

"What happens?"

"You and your stupid sperm are going to be the death of me!"

"My sperm?"

"Sperm!" Billy yells, raising his little hands in the air.

Caroline closes her eyes and pushes past me again, giving Billy his sippy cup. "Here, put this in your mouth, you cheeky little squirt." She winks at him and he grins up at her, that adoring smile on his face turning my heart to putty for a second.

But then I cross my arms with another frown. "What's wrong with my sperm?"

Her blue eyes hit me, her gaze bright and dangerous as she huffs and starts ranting, "They're thermonuclear! Or something! I mean what the hell, Casey? Do they just burn through the condoms?"

It takes me a second to figure out what she's telling me, and then my slow-ass brain finally gets it.

"Wait, you're pregnant?" An instant smile lights my face and can't even be tamped down by her smoldering glare.

She points her finger at me. "Don't you dare smile! I can't have three kids under four. Do you understand me? I can't do it." Her voice breaks, and all the rage that was fueling her disappears in an instant, fear washing over her face as her blue eyes fill with tears and her bottom lip starts to tremble. "I can't do it," she squeaks again, walking into my embrace and sniffling against my shoulder.

I brush my hand down her curls and hold her close. "Yes, baby, you can. You're an amazing mom." I pull back so I can look at her face. Cupping her cheeks, I can't help smiling again. "We're gonna have another kid. This is awesome! At this rate, we'll have our own hockey team. Your dad will love it."

"No way!" She shoves me back, totally missing my joke—which, I admit, might be slightly bad timing on my part, but come on! I'm gonna be a dad again! Excitement buzzes through me as Caroline's anger flares again.

"A hockey team?" She bulges her eyes at me. "I am not pushing that many heads out of my vagina!"

"Vagina!" Billy yells, and Troy raises his hand and says, "Ba-bah!"

I crack up laughing, which sets the boys into fits of giggles. Caroline's expression crumples again, and I can't decide if she's on the verge of sobbing or laughing along with us.

Stepping back into her space, I brush my thumb beneath her eyes, softening my voice and hopefully my expression. "I know it's scary right now, but it's going to be okay."

"How?" She blinks, sucking in a shaky breath.

"You're strong and amazing. I mean it when I say that you're the best mom. You can do this. *We* can do this."

She closes her eyes, setting a few tears free.

I brush them off her cheeks as they fall, kissing her forehead, then wrapping her in a hug again. "Just think, baby. It might be a girl."

She goes stiff against me before leaning back, her lips parting as the glimmer of a smile lights her eyes. I splay my hand over her stomach.

"A little girl with red curls and big blue eyes."

Caroline lets out a watery laugh, placing her hand over mine. "Quiet and sweet?"

I can't promise that, but I can promise... "She'll be adorable, and we're gonna love her so much."

She sniffs and starts to nod before wincing. "And if it's a boy?"

"We're gonna love him too." I grin. "We'll have three little musketeers on our hands. It's gonna be great no matter what." Her lip starts to shake again, and I brush my thumb across it. "You can do this, baby."

Pulling her back into my arms, I start dancing around the kitchen, singing "Don't Worry Baby." I don't even know how I know that Beach Boys song, and I only remember the chorus, but I sing that over and over again, spinning Caroline around and swaying with her against me until she's laughing into my shoulder and the boys are clapping and giggling from their highchairs.

JANUARY

CHAPTER 4
LEILANI

"You're pregnant? Again? You know how birth control works, right?" I can't help teasing my best friend as I stare at her through my phone and shake my head. Tammy, who's also on the call, stifles a laugh by covering her mouth.

I wink at her, then glance over my shoulder when I hear someone walk past my alcove. I've found a quiet corner of the library to take this call because the office space I share with three other postgrads is too far away. Plus, I don't want them overhearing my conversation. I doubt Caroline wants this news spread across the Nolan U campus, even though most of the student body won't even know who she is. She graduated three years ago.

"Okay, shut up. We did use protection, and it failed." She rolls her eyes "Again!"

"Ouch." Tammy winces. "No wonder you're reeling."

Caroline and Tammy share understanding smiles while I interject. "I bet Casey's excited, though."

"He's over the moon. Of course he is. He loves being a dad more than anything. He also doesn't have to grow anything in his stomach and then push it out, so he's got that going for him."

Tammy laughs. "Hopefully your parents can help out a little more while you're pregnant... and after the baby's born."

"Yeah, I'm sure they will." Caroline cringes. "They're thrilled, and possibly worried that Casey and I have way too much sex. If there is such a thing." She smirks, wriggling her eyebrows.

I bite my lips together, trying not to laugh. She and Casey have always had a very physical relationship. It's what brought them together in the first place.

"So, are you going to find out the gender or—" The phone beeps, and I grin, adding Mikayla to the call. "Hey, Mick."

She waves at me, looking slightly distracted as she shuffles papers on her desk. "Hey, guys, I've only got a sec. What's the big news?"

Caroline blows a curl off her cheek and tells her, "I'm pregnant."

"Again? What, are you birthing an army?"

"Shut up." Caroline laughs, then whines, "You guys! Why am I even telling you?"

"Because we're your besties and you love us." Mikayla gives her a pointed look, her left eyebrow arching.

Tammy giggles. "How far along are you?"

"I found out in November but wanted to wait and tell you guys once I got through the first trimester."

I frown. "Why'd you wait so long? I've been talking to you almost every week, and you've been sitting silent on this thing?"

"I'm sorry." She cringes. "I don't know... maybe I wanted to make sure it stuck." She shrugs, then looks all pained again. "Or maybe I was a little embarrassed that once again I'm accidentally pregnant. None of my babies have been planned. It's like the universe is giving me no say in how my life is gonna work out."

"I know." My voices softens as I feel her pain. I totally understand not having control of your life and how unsettling that can be. "I thought you wanted more than two kids, though."

"I did, but not all squished together this way." Caroline bulges her eyes. "I just wanted a year to breathe and not have a newborn or be pregnant. I have no idea how I'm supposed to manage three kids under four. Two takes nearly everything out of me, and the pregnancy exhaustion is next level. I'm freaking out."

"Maybe the universe knows that deep in your heart, you want to be a mama." Tammy's voice is gentle and kind.

Caroline goes a little misty-eyed. "I do love my babies. They're just a lot sometimes, you know? And the idea of being outnumbered three to one is terrifying."

"You're gonna be great. You're a tough, strong boss bitch. You can handle anything," Mikayla says.

"And you've still got months to get mentally prepared for this shift." I do some quick calculations in my head. "The baby must be due in July, right?"

"Yeah." She sniffs, then pouts. "I'm going to be the size of a blimp for your wedding, Tammy."

"You'll still look stunning." She smiles.

And I quickly assure my friend, "You always glow when you're pregnant."

Caroline scoffs and shakes her head.

"At least you haven't been puking up a lung like Tammy did, right?" Mikayla laughs, and Tammy joins her.

"Thank God that's over."

Our phones all bleep in unison, and I quickly add Rachel to the call.

"Sorry I'm late, ladies. Emergency in the kitchen." She fluffs her bangs and looks a little flustered as she smiles and waves at each person on the chat.

"All good, though?" Tammy checks.

"Yeah, just my new assistant chef, who I took pity on and maybe shouldn't have taken pity on, because training her is turning into quite the mission." Her expression buckles. "I just felt so bad for her in the interview, you know? She was so nervous and twitchy and sweet and..." She pulls a face. "And now the kitchen reeks of burnt cream."

"Oh no." I give her a sympathetic smile. "I'll be home around four. I can help you air the place out."

"You're an angel." She blows me a kiss.

"I can't believe you guys are still living in the pool house," Mikayla comments.

I feign insult with a little scoff. "It's the same size as your apartment in Centennial."

"In what universe?" Mikayla shakes her head with a laugh. "We have two bedrooms and an office. You're in like a studio."

"That Baxter has been expanding for us," I correct her. "You just haven't seen the completed renovations yet. When are you coming to visit, anyway? You've canceled the last two times."

She huffs and digs her fingers into her hair. "Work is crazy busy, and between Ethan's hockey schedule, my asshole boss, and his list of needy, demanding clients, I barely have a second to breathe. Who knew being a gopher could be so damn stressful." As if to prove her point, her work phone starts ringing, and she checks it with a growl. "I'm sorry, guys. I've gotta go. Congrats, Caroline!"

She hangs up, and Rachel looks a little mystified. "Why are we congratulating Caroline?"

There's an uncomfortable pause, Caroline's face paling slightly as she admits, "I'm pregnant again."

Rachel blinks, her lips parting as she struggles to hide her reaction.

She's gutted, and we can all feel her pain as we watch her fight to pull a smile into place.

"Wow." She swallows, her voice on the shaky side. "Amazing. So happy for you."

"Yeah, thanks." Caroline's expression crumples. "It wasn't planned. I'm just..." She winces and quickly mumbles, "I'm just trying not to freak out about having three kids under four."

"Billy will turn four just after the baby's born, won't he?" I try to keep my voice light and upbeat, desperate to end this heavy feeling that's taken over the call.

"Great. So now I have to plan a birthday party with a newborn. Thanks, Lani. That makes me feel way better." Her voice is snippy, and I know she instantly regrets it.

I wave off her apologetic look with a smile.

"You're blessed, Caroline. Don't forget that." Rachel's eyes fill; it's obvious even through my small screen. My heart starts to ache for her all over again. She's been trying to have kids ever since she and Liam got married four years ago. "Hey, um... sorry to cut this short, but I've got to go and deal with this kitchen thing and..." She shakes her head and sniffs. "Um, see you later."

She hangs up just as a baby starts crying in the background.

"That's my little Supernova," Tammy says. "Naptime's over. Better run. Nice to see you." She blows a kiss at the screen, then disappears, leaving just me and Caroline to lament the sad ending to what should have been a super joyful call.

Caroline groans. "Did you see Rachel's face?"

"I know," I murmur. "She wants to be a mama so bad."

"I don't get the universe sometimes!" Her voice pitches. "I just have to look at Casey's dick and I'm knocked up. Poor Ray's been trying for years now. It's not fair."

"I know. Thankfully, she's married to Liam, who is the sweetest, kindest man. Somehow they'll get through."

"Yeah." Caroline looks about ready to cry. "Do you think I should keep my distance while I go through this pregnancy? What do I do?"

"Well, thankfully you don't live in the same town, but..." I shrug. "You can't avoid her altogether. We're a family, and it wouldn't be right to ice either of you out."

"I just want to protect her." She swipes a tear off her face. "If being around me is too painful, then I'll back off."

"Why don't you just ask what she needs from you and be fine with whatever she says?"

"Yeah." Caroline nods, then sighs. "I'll do that. Good idea." Rubbing her forehead, she glances at her watch. "Troy's due to wake in a few minutes, and I have to collect Billy from preschool soon, so give me a quick update on your life. Go."

I laugh and tell her about my studies. "My dissertation is coming along beautifully. The small groups I'm teaching are mostly divine. My adviser is still super strict and grumpy, but I know she only wants the best for me. Even though I don't love her serious lack of people skills, she forces me to produce top-quality work, so I really can't fault her for that."

"How are you finding the workload?"

"Manageable. It helps that Asher has learned how to cook a few decent meals, and he's been keeping our place so tidy. I seriously love that man."

"Then marry him." Caroline singsongs like she always does.

"I know." I laugh. "I will."

"When?"

I glance away from her pointed look and hitch my shoulder. "I don't know."

"Why are you even hesitating over this? He's your soulmate. You've admitted that to me multiple times. And I know you believe in marriage, so what's the problem?"

"It's the wedding," I blurt. "The idea of some huge fiasco is just too much. I don't want to plan some big thing."

"Then don't. Just get married in a courthouse."

"Wow." I tip my head with a deadpan expression. "That's so romantic."

"Come on." Caroline rolls her eyes. "If you don't want a big wedding, then what do you want?"

"I'm not sure."

"You are impossible sometimes, you know that?" My best friend pulls a face, then laughs. "You know Asher is dying to marry you."

"And his parents will put on some elaborate show, and my army of a family will all want to be there."

"It doesn't have to be this big thing."

I tut, knowing she's right but not wanting to admit it. "We're basically married anyway. We've been living together for three years."

"I know, but it's not the same. There's just something about making it official that's so special." Caroline touches her heart. "I love being Mrs. Pierce."

My eyebrow arches. "I'm not changing my last name."

"You don't have to, but putting a ring on it is fun, Lani. You can't tell me that a small part of you doesn't want some whopping great diamond on your hand."

I wrinkle my nose, and Caroline laughs again.

"Let Asher propose to you already."

"Why should *he* get to propose?"

"Fine!" She throws her hand up with an exasperated smile. "You propose to him, then! Just put a freaking ring on it already!"

I grin at her expression, the idea sparking something playful and warm inside of me.

I *could* propose to him.

You know, that could be kind of fun. And as for the wedding thing... well, maybe I can handle it.

Asher is my soulmate. I have no doubts about that.

And the expression on his face if I popped the question...

I bite my lip, giddy butterflies swarming me as I let that scenario play out in my imagination.

"Oh, that's good," I whisper to myself. "That is really good."

CHAPTER 5
LIAM

I spin my wedding ring around, staring at the gold band and trying to harden myself against the wails coming from the house to my right. I'm standing on the front lawn of this small residence, there as backup for the social worker who is removing two kids from a dangerous situation.

This sucks.

Glancing at my partner, we share a cringing frown as the mother starts screaming.

"Get your hands off my babies! Leave them the fuck alone! Don't you touch them! Don't you touch them!"

I adjust my police belt, gripping the sides while the social worker calmly explains, "Ma'am, we've been over this. I need to take them for a while. You'll be able to visit. They'll be safe and well cared for."

"My babies!" She's wailing as Denise walks out the front door with a baby in her arms and two kids with big eyes and bony arms trailing after her. Their threadbare coats can't hide how skinny they are. The little boy looks terrified, and I feel sick as I take in the bruises around his neck. His big sister doesn't look much better, with purple-and-blue marks on her cheek and chin. She holds his hand and tugs him along.

"Come on." She pulls him forward. "Don't look."

"No! Stop!" The mother rushes out after them, and I'm forced to step forward, catching the bat she's wildly swinging.

The girl ducks, shielding her brother, while Denise spins with a gasp, ushering the children forward. "It's okay. It's okay. Kids, follow me."

The boy starts crying, and I want to pull him into a hug and promise him the world won't hurt him again.

But I can't do that.

Since becoming a police officer, I've come to realize the world—even a small town like Nolan—can be a very dark and dangerous place.

"No! Stop them!" The woman looks at me, but I doubt she can see my face properly. Her pupils are dilated, her breaths short and punchy. She's high. And from the report I read on the way over here, I know it's meth running through her system.

It breaks my heart as I lower her to the ground, rolling her onto her stomach so I can cuff her. She screams into the icy pavement, shouting for her children while I keep a gentle hand on her shoulder so she can't rear up and attack me.

My partner stands watch while I keep her still, making sure the kids get into the vehicle safely.

I try to keep my touch light and calm, even when she gets a surge of energy and starts battling me. She doesn't know what she's doing right now, and when she crashes and finds her kids gone... she'll be wrecked.

Turning back with a sad sigh, Caleb helps me get the woman to her feet and we walk her to the squad car, securing her in the back before radioing the station.

The booking goes as smoothly as it can, and I manage to write up most of my report before heading back out on patrol, cruising the streets past Nolan U campus and making sure the college kids are behaving themselves. It only feels like yesterday since I was one of them. My carefree days of hockey and classes... it was a good life.

Damn, we thought we were so smart, owning life and dominating on the ice.

But we didn't know shit.

Not really.

Adulting is hard. It's good hard. I love my life. But some days in this job are tougher than others, and I'm feeling it today. Abused kids are always a trigger for me. Probably because I was one. I've worked my way through it, but every time I have to deal with a case like today, it rears its head and I'm back to going through the steps.

At least it's quicker than it used to be. I find my calm, peaceful place with relative ease, and Caleb's none the wiser as he navigates down Main Street and turns east.

My phone dings, and I check the message, my heart sinking as I read Casey's text.

It's announcement day! Baby number three is on the way! My house is turning into a zoo but bring it on!

"Shit," I mutter, staring at the string of happy emojis that would usually make me laugh. But all I can think about is Rachel.

Does she know yet?

"You good, man?" Caleb glances at me.

"Yeah, just need to call my wife. Can you pull over, please?"

He does so without hesitation, and I jump out of the car, calling Rachel and holding my breath until she answers.

"Hey."

I can instantly tell she's been crying, and my heart starts bleeding.

"Cariño." I whisper her pet name, and she breaks down.

Squeezing my forehead, I keep my emotions in check, not wanting her to carry the burden of my own pain too.

Ever since she told me she wanted to have kids, I've been all in. She whispered it to me on our wedding night, and we started trying on our honeymoon. Yeah, we were young, but I was so ready to build a family with this woman. She was going to be an amazing mother. Her sweet heart and kind smile... I couldn't wait to watch her interacting with our babies.

But... they never came.

It's been about four years, and we've had no luck.

Every month she gets her period.

And every month, she cries.

Now Caroline's pregnant and—

"I'm fine," she whimpers. "Thanks for calling to check on me, but really... you need to focus on your shift. You be safe, and I'll... I'll see you when you get home." She squeaks out the last few words, then hangs up before I can say anything.

Leaning against the hood of the car, I feel my chest deflate, my insides concaving as I lightly kick a clump of snow on the path.

"Hey, man. Everything all right?" Caleb's head pops out the window.

I glance over my shoulder, trying to smile at my partner. He's older than me, with twin girls in middle school and years' worth of experience on the force.

"Just..." I hold up my phone, then make myself stand. "Rachel's having a really bad day. She's crying and..." I shake my head.

He gives me a kind smile. "Think it's about time you clock out for the day, then, huh?"

I glance at my watch. "I've still got three hours before my shift ends."

"No, you don't. Family always comes first. I'll clear it

with Sarge." He tips his head, quietly ordering me back into the squad car.

I do as I'm told, and forty minutes later, I'm pulling into my parking spot behind Ponderosa.

Walking into the mudroom, I pause to take off my shoes, wondering what that funky smell is in the kitchen. With a wrinkled nose, I step in to find Asher and the chef who covers Rachel's shift three nights a week hovering near the stove.

"What happened in here?" I ask.

"Burnt cream," the chef mutters, shaking his head. "Such a waste. Ray needs to fire that new assistant. She knows it. I know it." He bulges his eyes and I wince, then cast my gaze to Asher.

"Where is she?"

He gives me a sad smile. "I convinced her to go take a shower."

"Was she wrecked?"

Asher nods. "Yeah, man."

I close my eyes, taking in a deep breath before thanking the chef for coming in early and Asher for helping us out.

"Anytime." He waves me off. "Go take care of your woman."

I rush up to the top floor. Since everyone moved out, we've turned this level into our own space. Baxter converted the end room into a living area for us, and we have our master bedroom plus a couple spares. One was supposed to be a nursery. We had grand plans of having two kids close together. Rachel was excited to have them sharing a room, then turning the other one into a playroom for them.

But that never happened. For the first year, we were okay. I was at the police academy anyway, and we figured the timing wasn't quite right. Then I had to get through being a rookie, but Rachel wanted to start trying again anyway, so we did.

And we haven't stopped.

It's been over two years of maximum effort and zero results.

I find Ray sitting on the toilet lid, wrapped in a towel and crying. Her bare shoulders shake, her wet hair sticking to her back as she weeps into her hands.

I crouch in front of her, resting my hands lightly on her knees. She knows it's me so doesn't bother looking up. Instead, she sniffles into her palms and hiccups out the words. "I got my period this morning, and then Sadie burned the cream, and then... Caroline called."

"I'm sorry, baby."

"She's..."

"I know."

Looking at me with her big green eyes, I feel like my heart is breaking all over again. It does this every month and somehow repairs itself just in time to crack in new places.

"Why isn't this working for us?" she squeaks. "Caroline doesn't even want to be pregnant, and I'm desperate for a baby. How is that fair?"

I rest my hand on her head, lightly kissing the tears off her cheeks. "I know it sucks. And I'm sorry the IVF hasn't worked." Going through that was an expensive, harrowing experience and not one we want to repeat in a hurry. Rachel found it physically and emotionally draining. It was a mental struggle for me too, and the only time we've ever yelled at each other was when we were in the middle of that shitstorm. Listening to Rachel's heartbroken sobs when she locked herself away in the bathroom nearly killed me.

We got through it, and were probably stronger afterward, but I never want to go through that again. Raising my voice at my woman that way? It's not me. I don't want to be that guy.

The doctor did say we could try IVF again in the future, but I just can't bring myself to suggest it.

My heart sinks.

Rachel shakes her head, her chest heaving as she obviously tries to rein in her tears. "We can never say we didn't try. I just..." Her expression crumples. "When we got married, I had this picture in my mind, you know? You, me, a few kids. Teaching them how to bake and catch a ball. Taking them to hockey games so they can watch their Uncle Ethan and Uncle Casey play. You showing them how to skate." She starts to cry again.

"I want that too." I touch her hair, my voice hitching at her anguished tears.

This is killing me.

Wrapping my arm around her waist, I catch her

against me, and we tip to the floor. Resting my back against the wall, I cradle her on my knee, smoothing her hair and letting her cry into my shirt.

I don't say anything for a long time. Not until her tears have dried up and she's down to soft whimpers. Brushing my lips across her forehead, I rub my hand down her back and gently suggest, "Maybe it's time we seriously consider adoption."

She goes still and sniffs. "Yeah. Maybe." Her long fingers play with the buttons of my shirt. "I guess I just wanted a little part of you and a little part of me all blended together. But that's never going to happen, is it?"

I curl my hand around hers. "Whether they're our blood or not, they'd still be ours, and we'd love them with everything we've got."

Pulling in a shaky breath, she sits up, her eyes glistening as she gives me a closed-mouth smile. "Yeah, we would." Her head starts bobbing. "We'd love them so much."

Cupping the back of her head, I pull her forward, crushing our mouths together, then holding her tight, quietly praying that we'll get this chance to become parents.

I want to raise kids with this woman.

I want to watch her be a mama.

I want to live my life with her by my side, and I want to see her smile every day.

I'll do whatever it takes to make her happy. Whatever I possibly can.

MARCH

CHAPTER 6
ETHAN

Careening down the rink, I get myself in position to receive the puck, quickly gathering it and flicking it off to my right. We've practiced this play a million times over, and when it shoots back to me, I send it toward the net. Holding my breath, I watch it fly, skimming the goalie's shoulder before whacking into the back of the net.

"Fuck yeah!" I punch the air while the fans in the arena go nuts. It's not the roar of a Colorado crowd, but there are enough people here cheering us on.

My teammates skate toward me, smacking me on the helmet as we celebrate the goal together.

We've got three minutes left in the game, and if we can defend our goal, we're going to win this. Yes! I can taste the Stanley Cup playoffs. At this rate, we'll make first round, and I can't fucking wait!

I'm living out my dreams right now, and I'm pumped.

Coach pulls me off rotation and I jump into the box,

cheering on my team as they keep our goal clean and nearly score again. The buzzer sounds and we erupt, jumping back onto the ice and celebrating the win.

This was an epic battle, and we're high on adrenaline as we pile on top of one another. Casey's pounding me on the back and laughing. "Yaaassss! We did it, man! We fucking did it!"

I slap his helmet, giddy with this triumph.

An away game against one of the strongest teams in the league. We're going to be celebrating tonight!

We finally skate off the ice, enduring interviews as we make our way to the lockers. I say all the things I'm supposed to say, playing it cool while itching to get out of my sweaty gear and call my wife. She said she was going to be watching the game. I wanted her here with me, but work has taken over her life, so it's hard to pin her down.

I try not to complain, but it riles me pretty bad.

I miss the days when she'd make herself available to me.

Now I'm slotted in, and as much as I want her to progress and succeed in her career... a selfish part of me wishes she wasn't so fucking motivated. I miss my girl. I miss looking into the stands and finding her pretty face.

I miss walking out of the arena and having her jump into my arms.

I thought when she finally graduated and we got married that things would be different. No more long-distance from Nolan to Centennial. And that first year, it was fucking awesome. But since she got this new job with the more impressive agency... it's sucked.

It's a strategic move on her part. Leave the smaller agency to advance up the food chain. But she's stepped down in position to get into this prestigious firm and is basically a gopher for this agent I can't stand. He's a total fuckwit, and the big boss above him isn't much better. She's at their beck and call and will drop anything to be anywhere and do anything.

It pisses me off to no end.

My lil' mouse is worth so much more than that, but do you think I can convince her?

She's determined to see this through and work her way up the ranks.

"This opportunity came to me, and I have to take it!" she argued the last time we fought about it.

"What about law school? What about becoming an agent? What about representing female athletes?"

"This job will get me there! I don't *have* to have a law degree to do this, okay?"

"You do if you want to represent pro athletes. You had a plan, Mick. You—"

"Plans change, okay? Ryan has assured me that he'll get me to where I want to be. I just have to put in my time and work my way up in the company."

Ryan. I fucking hate that guy.

I finally met him at the Christmas party last year and instantly didn't like him. He's smarmy and false, and I can't believe Mikayla doesn't see right through him. She's so desperate to make it that she's stopped seeing things clearly, and no matter how much I beg her to take notice, she won't.

I dump my stick and start unlacing my skates, my mood turning black as those around me celebrate our win. I try to smile along with them, but all I want to do is talk to Mick and celebrate with her. Damn, I wish she was here.

Snatching my phone out of my locker, I head to the back corner and call her. It's still noisy as hell, but I press my finger to my ear and wait for her to answer.

Which she doesn't.

"Hey, you've reached Mikayla Galloway. I'm not available to take your call right now. Please leave me a message, and I'll get back to you as soon as I can. Thanks."

I miss her old message, her voice bubbly and playful as she told whoever was calling that she was busy, and depending on the quality of your message, she might consider returning you call. Instead, I'm listening to this formal bullshit and missing her with an ache that's making me vile.

With a growl, I slam my phone back into my locker and stalk to the showers. I take my sweet time and eventually amble out of the locker room for another set of interviews before making my way back to the hotel.

Casey convinces me to join him at the bar, and I reluctantly go for drinks with all the other guys who are flying solo tonight. I down a beer while I listen to them go on about how great we played. I want to join them, but I can't stop looking at my phone and wondering why Mick hasn't called me back yet. I didn't leave a message, but she'll get a missed call notification.

Come on, baby. Where the fuck are you?

A few pretty women have joined us and are lounging on the single men's knees... and one married guy.

I see you, Lawson. You cheating asshole.

I watch the girls' glossy lips smile. The guys hold them close and laugh along with whatever they're saying. The sounds go muted around me, and I nearly miss Casey's voice. Actually, I do, until he nudges me in the arm and asks, "Who the fuck is that?"

I glance at his phone, snatching it out of his hand when I notice the guy standing next to Mick.

It's the agency's social media account, and my lil' mouse is standing beside a tall athlete, laughing at whatever he's saying, while Ryan is on her other side, his arm around her waist and his hand resting on her hip like she's with him and not *my* fucking wife!

I frown at the image, realizing quickly that it was only just posted. Now I know why she wasn't answering her phone before. She's busy schmoozing—her word, not mine. I glare at the three of them, torturing myself with every detail of the photo, until I spot something that makes my stomach twist into a sick knot.

"I'm out," I growl, thrusting Casey's phone back at him and jerking away from the table.

"You know the guy?" Casey calls after me.

"She works with him," I shout over my shoulder, practically snarling the words as I stalk to the elevator and head up to my room.

My blood is boiling by the time I swipe my keycard, and I swear to God, I'm—

The phone in my pocket starts buzzing and I wrench it out, swiping my thumb across the screen and spitting, "Well, I see you're having a busy night!"

"Yeah, sorry I missed your call, but congratulations on the win!" Mikayla's voice pitches with excitement, and I can't enjoy any of it.

Slumping onto the bed, I glare around my hotel suite, hating that she's not here with me. Hating that she's at some event with her sleazy colleagues and—

"I didn't manage to catch the whole game, but I saw your final goal and scared the crap out of the lady standing beside me when I cheered for you." She laughs, and I manage a soft snicker. At least she saw that part. It was my only goal of the game, and she saw it. That should make me happy, right?

"Where are you tonight?"

"Well…" She huffs. "I was supposed to be at home in my boxers and your hockey jersey watching the game and cheering you on, but I got a last-minute call from Ryan and had to drag my ass down to some party thing and schmooze a few athletes while being his personal gopher."

"Ryan does that a lot, huh," I grit out, failing to keep my voice calm and even.

She pauses, obviously picking up on my mood. "He sure does. I seriously don't know how the guy managed to get anything done before I came to work for him," she jokes, and I can't even muster a smile.

All I can see is that asshole's hand on her hip. All I can see is her ringless wedding finger resting against her stomach as she laughed at what was being said and—fuck! Do I call her on it?

I should shut my mouth and not get into a big fight, but I can't help myself.

"So, yeah, I've been stuck at this party thing and—"

"Looks like it's not the worst night of your life," I grumble.

"What?"

"Casey showed me a post. Looks like the schmoozing is going well."

"Ugh, really? Which picture did they post?" She puts me on speaker so she can check, and I direct her to the place I saw it. "Oh phew, that's not too bad. I look half decent. I don't even know why they include me in this stuff. I'm a nobody at the agency. Ryan just dragged me over to meet Jabari Williams. He's an up-and-comer in the basketball scene. The kid's got skills. It was kinda cool to meet him."

"Yeah, schmoozing your ass off, I see."

She goes quiet and I glare at the wall, waiting for it...

"Okay, what is your problem?" Her voice turns snappy. "This is my job. I have to do whatever these agents ask me to. We've talked about this. If I have to show up last minute at a party and talk sweet to some athletes, then I'll do it."

"The guy's got his hands all over you."

"What? No, he doesn't!" she snaps, then sighs. "Oh, you mean Ryan. Yeah, the guy's a little handsy, but it's nothing I can't handle."

"He's more than handsy. He's the most demanding agent you work with. He's always calling you out to last-minute stuff, and you go without argument."

"I have to. It's my job. He'll be the one writing my performance review."

"You work so much fucking overtime for that guy. He's taking advantage of you."

She lets out a tired sigh. "Look, a year or two of servitude is going to get me where I need to go. I just have to muscle through this phase, and if I can prove myself, then I'll start getting athletes assigned to me, and if I'm really good, they'll give me my own gopher who I will treat so much fucking better than Ryan treats me."

I scoff because I don't know what else to say.

"Come on, Ethan," Mick whines. "How many times do we have to have this conversation?"

I grit my teeth and shake my head. "Did he tell you not to wear your rings as well?"

She goes quiet again, and I can picture her face. She's either doing her guilty blush or her eyes are narrowing in anger.

Her voice is icy soft when she finally replies. "Yeah, I

was rushing out of the house, and I forgot to put them on."

"Why weren't you wearing them? I never take my ring off." I lift my hand, flicking the band with my thumbnail.

"Because you have a simple gold band. My rings are huge, okay? That diamond catches on everything. When I'm home, I take it off, and I wasn't expecting to have to get all dolled up and be running out the door tonight. It was a simple mistake."

"Uh-huh."

"Ethan," she warns me. "Don't be a douche about this. They all know I'm married to you. It's not a big deal."

"Yeah, I'm not sure Ryan's aware."

"Believe me, he's aware. You don't have to worry about anything with that idiot. Like I'd let him cross any kind of line. He's a colleague, that's it." She huffs. "I've got you. Why would I want anybody else?"

I roll my eyes and try to keep my voice calm and even. "I'm not worried about you cheating on me. I just hate the way that guy treats you. And I don't like him holding you in a photograph like you're his and not mine!"

Okay, so I'm losing the calm battle.

"I *am* yours. Always and forever, remember?" Mick tries to mollify me.

All I can do is grumble, "Yeah, well, doesn't look that way in the fucking photograph."

She grunts, and I can feel our argument escalating. I'm doing this. I'm fueling the fire, and I need to quit it and end this call on something nice, but I'm too riled for sweet sentiments. Instead, I clench my jaw and go quiet, willing myself not to say anything dumb.

"Ethan, you're the guy I married, okay? Don't read into one stupid photograph like it means everything. Ryan is a douche, but for now, I work for him, and I won't risk losing a great opportunity because you're feeling jealous. I'm sorry this photo is pissing you off, but you have to trust me."

"It's not just the photo. I tried calling you after the game and—"

"I was in the middle of a conversation and couldn't take your call right then. Jeez, I have a life outside your hockey career, Ethan. I'm not some hockey wife who can follow you around the country, like my only goal is to live off your wealth and be a pretty face by your side when you're leaving the arena."

"I'm not asking—"

"That would kill me, okay? And you knew that when you married me. I thought you wanted me to have a career of my own."

I squeeze my eyes shut and pinch my nose. "I do."

"But only if I can still be at your beck and call, right?"

"No, Mick, of course not! I just..."

"You just what? What do you want from me?" Her voice is getting snappier by the second, and I can't see things deescalating unless I wrap up this call.

I'd usually fight this out like we always do—get a little explosive and then work through it—but I don't think there's anything I can say right now that will get us moving forward.

So, I go for an easy out.

"Nothing," I murmur. "I guess I just miss you."

She sighs. "I miss you too. But you're home on Friday, right?"

"Yeah." I scrub a hand down my face. "I'll see you then."

"I love you."

"Yeah, love you too."

We say it, but it doesn't really sound like we mean it— two grumpy-ass voices muttering the L-word before hanging up.

Is she still feeling as pissed off as I am?

Slumping back on the bed, I drop my phone and stare at the ceiling, a flash of worry coursing through me.

Fuck.

I feel like I'm losing my wife, and I don't know how to stop this thing from falling apart.

CHAPTER 7
ASHER

"Hey, man! I watched the game. It was epic. Your goal at the end was perfect execution." I grin and start to laugh. "You know how much it kills me to give your ass a compliment, bro, so you know it was good hockey."

Ethan laughs, but the sound isn't as bright as I was expecting.

"You okay?" I ask, holding up a finger to tell the person waiting for me that I'll just be a minute.

"Yeah."

I make a game show buzzer noise. "Wrong answer, folks. Contestant number one is obviously lying."

Ethan snickers, and I can picture him shaking his head.

"You didn't come away with some kind of delayed injury or anything, did you?"

"Nah, it's..." He sighs and mutters, "Fuck. I just got in

a fight with Mick last night. Still unresolved, and it's eating me big-time."

"What happened?"

"I'll spare you the details, but we're just... not on the same page right now."

I frown. That's unusual. Those two are usually so in sync. Although, Lani felt like something was a little off at the New Year's party a few months back.

"Anything I can help with?"

"No." Ethan's probably shaking his head again, squaring his shoulders, ready to tough it out with zero support.

"You know I'm here for you, right? We all are. If there's anything we can do..."

"Yeah, I know, thanks. But this is between me and Mick. We'll figure it out. Anyways, I gotta go. Got a session with my PT."

"Okay. Good luck with tomorrow's game, yeah?"

"Thanks, man. I'll catch you later."

We hang up and I stare at my phone for a minute, troubled by the call. It's not my business, but trouble in paradise for Mick and Ethan sucks. Those two have been solid since his junior year at college. I mean, sure, they argue and bicker like Lani and I do, but they've always worked through their issues. I've never heard Ethan so rattled before, and it's weirding me out.

"Asher, you ready?"

I glance up and smile at my potential client, rushing

over to the table and ordering us drinks before starting the initial meeting.

It goes well. I love his business idea, and I think it's got potential. I give him some tips and guidance around starting up a small business and offer my services. He's going to let me know next week.

Feeling confident that I'll be taking on another client, I walk to my car with a smile and check the time. Lani should be finishing up with her classes soon, and we're going to spend the evening together. Damn, I wish she was my wife. I've mentioned marriage a bunch of times, but she's kept putting me off, telling me she needs to get through her studies first.

I get that.

I've been building up my business, too, and it's all very time-consuming. The idea of planning a wedding as well is a little too much.

But damn... I wish she was my wife.

Pulling away from Main Street, I head into an older suburb of Nolan, figuring I'll use up the last hour of my day by checking in on Baxter. He's working a renovation on an old house that sustained some fire damage in the kitchen. Initially, when he started up Baxter's Got You Covered, he was taking on small jobs here and there—an interior repaint, hanging wallpaper, cleaning out guttering. But after he renovated the pool house for us, I used it to his advantage, doing a marketing push, and managed to score him some bigger jobs. I think he prefers it, and it brings in a decent income for him too.

Parking behind his van, I lock the car and head inside.

"Bax, you in, man?"

"Yeah, back here!"

I follow the sound of music and find him in the kitchen, nailing in a fresh sheet of drywall. I step around his equipment and help him hold it, even though he probably doesn't need me to, while he uses the nail gun to quickly attach the wood.

Running my hand over it, I gaze around his progress.

"You're doing good."

"Yeah, no hitches yet. If things keep going this smoothly, I should be done by the end of the month." He throws me a cynical smile. "But when do things ever go without a hitch, right?"

"True." I laugh. "But you always manage to work your way through it."

"What's the time?" He hitches his tool belt before pulling out his tape measure.

"Close to three. You on school pickup today?"

"Shit, yeah. I am."

"Want me to do it?"

"Nah." Baxter starts closing windows and securing the house. "Kai's got hockey practice anyway, and I'm his coach this year."

His smile is big, pride for his stepson shining through strong.

"He's having a killer year."

"Right? At the rate he's going, he might just become a Cougar."

I laugh. "If he wants that."

"Yeah, I know… Tammy keeps telling me to stop pushing and let him get there on his own, but just between you and me, I'll be gutted if he gives up the game. He's too good."

"I'm sure he'll keep loving it just as much as we all did. I'm hoping to come to his game on Saturday."

"And this is why I love you." Baxter winks at me, and we walk out of the house together. "Is Lani coming too? Tammy will be there. I'm sure she'd love the company."

"Yeah, I'll ask her. Workload has been amping up, but she might be able to squeeze in a game."

"Good." Baxter nods.

"How are the wedding plans going?" I slide my hands into my pockets as he unlocks the van and loads his stuff inside.

He laughs. "Not bad. It's just been a matter of booking stuff, so that's relatively easy. I'm not having to make any high-pressure decisions like the first time around."

I smooth back my hair, which the wind keeps insisting on ruffling. "I can't decide if planning a wedding sounds like fun or a nightmare."

"I guess it depends on if you're dealing with a bridezilla, which Tammy is most definitely not." He slides the van door shut and turns to me with a smile. "I got so lucky."

I grin. "We all did."

"So, when are you gonna get off your ass and ask the Hawaiian Hottie to marry you? That woman is pure gold and you know it."

"I do know it, but she's not ready yet, and I want to respect that."

"Is she really not, though?" He gives me a skeptical frown.

I shrug. "She says she wants to wait until after she's finished with school. She's got about a year left."

"Yeah, I'm not buying it. Getting married while you're studying does not have to be this big thing. I think you've both built the idea of a wedding into this huge, impossible task when it can be as simple as saying 'I do.'"

"True." I nod yet want to argue that he doesn't have my mother, who will want to turn it into a *New York Times* front-page event.

"And who says you have to get married right away? You could at least propose and put a ring on her finger, you know?"

"I have thought about it," I admit, following Baxter around to his side of the van so we can finish our conversation.

"Yeah?" He grins at me. "How would you propose?"

"I've had some ideas. A fancy night out in Denver and a flower-filled penthouse suite. Or maybe I'd get down on one knee in the elevator." A secret smile touches my lips as memories from our first date in Denver flood me.

Baxter gives me a questioning frown, and I quickly shake my head, clearing my throat and continuing, "Or maybe flying her to the beach for a weekend and writing *will you marry me* in the sand. But she'll figure out what I'm up to if I pull something that big." I rest my shoulder against the van. "More than anything, I'd just love to surprise her, you know?"

"Then maybe popping the question a year early, when she least suspects it, is the way to go." He wiggles his eyebrows. "Proposing in your pajamas over breakfast can be just as meaningful as some fancy-ass dinner, dude. Just ask her already."

I grin at him, kind of loving the idea of mixing things up and doing something Lani will never see coming. My brain starts ticking over with a batch of new ideas as I wave goodbye to Baxter and head back to the Ponderosa villa.

CHAPTER 8
RACHEL

I wrap my fingers around my coffee mug and smile at Lani. I'm so glad she could meet me today. She's been so busy with classes and her dissertation, she hasn't had much time to spare. But when I told her I was in town, she offered to meet me for coffee.

We've managed to secure the corner couches at Java Jeans, and even though I'm only twenty-four, I'm feeling ancient as I watch these college students traipse in and out the door.

Lani smiles and waves at a few of them.

"Students," she murmurs before sipping her coffee, then breaking off a piece of muffin. "So, how's the adoption thing going?"

"Well, we've started the process." I bulge my eyes. "I had no idea how much paperwork there was to deal with. So many forms, plus interviews. They really vet you hard."

"Any hiccups?"

"Everything has mostly gone okay. We got an adoption grant, which covers two-thirds of the cost." I grin, a thrill buzzing through me over how easily that all came together. It was like a little miracle. Like the universe was telling us we're on the right track. "We had a home visit the other day and their only big concern is our living situation. I don't think they're too keen on us raising a baby on the top floor of a bed-and-breakfast." I frown. "I know it's unconventional. Liam and I are trying to figure out what to do. We can't really afford to buy a house yet. I mean, we could find a little rental somewhere, I guess, but—"

"Why don't you move into the pool house? It's got that cute little yard out back, and now that Baxter's finished the renovations, it's plenty big enough for a small family."

"But you and Asher live in there."

"We can move upstairs. That way, you're in a separate living space, which is way more conventional, and it's farther from the guests."

"That's true." I tip my head. "You sure you wouldn't mind that, though?"

"Not at all. The noise doesn't travel up there too badly, does it?"

"No, I tend to put couples on the floor just below us and families go below them, so things are usually pretty quiet on the top floor, and I trust you and Asher not to crash around and disturb our guests..." My expression crumples. "I just don't want to inconvenience you guys."

"It's really not a big deal." She grins, and I love her more today than I did yesterday.

"Thank you so much. That would be amazing."

"I'll obviously double-check with Asher, but I'm sure he won't mind. Are there any other factors that are making the adoption agency hesitant?"

I take another sip of coffee, draining my mug before setting it down on the coffee table. "I think they're also worried about me working long hours while trying to raise a kid. They know that Liam's a police officer and I manage the villa, plus run the kitchen."

"Yeah, but you're not in sole charge. Plus, you could hire someone to make the team a little bigger. You could also ask Alonso if he'd be willing to be on call sometimes so it's not always on you. That way, when Liam's on night shift, you can focus solely on the baby and not have to worry about it. That's no big deal at all."

I purse my lips, thinking it through. "Alonso only lives five minutes away. That's a really good suggestion."

"Plus, Asher lives on-site, and you know how much he loves to jump in and help when there's an emergency." She winks and laughs, obviously loving that about him.

"You're probably right about hiring another person to help in the kitchen, though. That would definitely lighten my load." I wince. "Although, I'll need Asher's help in picking someone. I totally screwed up with my last hire."

She gives me a kind smile, reaching forward to pat my arm. "That's because you have such a gentle heart."

"I couldn't bring myself to fire her." I cringe, then tip my head back. "Thank God she quit."

"Yeah, well, maybe she could see the writing on the wall." Lani bulges her eyes, and we both end up laughing.

Relief pulses through me at how I dodged that bullet. Conflict is so not my forte. I wish I had some of Mikayla's fire or Lani's ability to put people in their place. She has this way of being so elegantly cutting when she wants to be. I would love to be able to stay that composed and assertive at the same time.

She really is a phenomenal woman. All of my friends are wonderful. I never thought moving to Nolan would expand my friend group this way, but Mick and I have found such a home with these people, and each new person who came into Hockey House just seemed to fit.

My eyes dart to the coffee table as I think about Caroline and how I haven't spoken to her since she announced her pregnancy. Shit. I am such a bad friend. I totally ghosted her back in January. Even after guilt got the better of me, I couldn't find the courage to return her call, and since then I've been busy with the adoption stuff. I need to get over myself and check on her.

Chewing my bottom lip, I wrinkle my nose and glance at Lani.

"Hey, um... how's Caroline doing?"

Lani gives me a gentle smile. "She's good. Things are busy with the kids and..." She hesitates and I nod, gripping my mug and willing myself to ask.

"And the pregnancy?"

"Baby and mama are both healthy."

"Cool." I bob my head, then stop when I notice Lani's pained expression. "What?"

"They're having a girl."

"Really?" I sit up with a smile. "Wow, she must be so happy."

"She is."

"Then why are you frowning?"

"I just feel bad that... she didn't tell you. I mean, she wanted to, but she's so aware of your situation, and she hasn't wanted to upset you."

Guilt simmers through me. "I get it. She's been so understanding, and I'm grateful. I need to... call her or something. I've been a terrible friend."

"No." Lani reaches for me, shuffling on the couch so she can sit closer. "Don't say that. She understands, and she's not mad at you over it. She just wishes this could be happening for you too. She knows how badly you want kids. She gets that her accidentally getting pregnant must be a punch to the gut for someone who has been trying for so long."

I blink, unbidden tears quickly rising. I fight them off as best I can.

"I'm sure she'd appreciate a phone call from you when you're ready. Maybe you could tell her about the adoption and stuff."

"Who knows how long that's going to take," I murmur, not wanting to be a pessimist but also trying to be realistic.

"Yeah, well, good things take time." Lani squeezes my wrist.

I glance at her, loving how caring she is and needing to end our coffee catch-up on a better note. She has to go soon, and I can't have us shuffling out of here all down in the dumps.

How can I brighten things up?

Changing the subject is a must, but...

"What's going on?" Lani frowns at me.

"Huh?"

"You have this look on your face like you want to tell me something, but you're not sure if you should."

"Oh. No." I shake my head with a soft laugh. "I was just wanting to end things on a better note and was scrambling to think of a subject change."

Her brown gaze softens with understanding. "It's okay to be sad. We can share that together. I'm here for you... whatever mood you're in."

"I know." I grab her hand in appreciation. "But I don't want to walk out of here with a gray cloud hanging over me, so let's talk about something uplifting, like... weddings or... proposals or—" I quickly swallow, silently cursing my stupid mouth.

Lani gives me a questioning frown. "Proposals?"

Of course she was going to pick up on that. I couldn't have just shut up after saying the word *weddings*? We could be talking about Baxter and Tammy right now, about how we're both bridesmaids. We could be planning another bachelorette party for our friend. But no, of course I had to say *proposals*, and she had to notice that I said the P-word, and now she's wondering who I'm talking about and—

"How did you know I was thinking of proposing to Asher? I haven't told anyone."

"What?" I whip around to gape at her. "You are?"

"Ye-ah." She drags out the word and points at me. "What are you talking about?"

"Nothing," I squeak.

"Rachel." Lani's teacher voice is just a touch scary, and I end up swallowing.

Then I quickly blurt, "The fact that Tammy told me that Baxter told her that Asher wants to surprise you with a proposal."

Lani goes still, blinking for a second, before crossing her arms with a sly smile. "Does he now?"

I gasp, my eyes bulging. "I'm so dead if he finds out that I let it slip! You can't tell him that you know!"

Her smirk grows a little bigger, her eyes gleaming. "He's trying to surprise me, huh?"

"Yes." I wince, then grab her wrist. "You can act surprised, right? Just pretend I didn't say anything."

"Or I could surprise him first." Her sharp gaze zeros in on my face. "Do you know when he's planning to propose?"

I shake my head, panic coursing through me at what I might have just started. Why did I say anything?

Ugh!

Lani's eyes are sparking with determination as her

phone dings. She checks the screen, then jolts from her seat. "I've gotta run. A student is waiting to see me about his assignment. But I'll catch you again soon."

"Okay." I give her a nervous smile. "You won't give away the fact that I told you about Asher's surprise?"

"No way." She grins, lightly kissing my cheek. "I'm grateful."

"But..."

She walks away before I can say anything else.

Crap.

Slumping back in my seat, I frown at my empty coffee mug and close my eyes. All I can hope is that I haven't gone and rocked too many boats with my little slipup.

CHAPTER 9
MIKAYLA

"And Galloway slips up, missing that shot by a mile. What is going through his head right now?" The commentator's voice is starting to grate as I watch my man skate around the back of the goal with a frustrated frown.

"Come on, baby. You can do this." I chew my thumbnail, watching the game on my phone because I'm supposed to be working, and my boss will be pissed if he catches me cheering on my husband when I should be proofing the contract on my desk for spelling and grammar.

At first I was stoked when he started giving me that job. I felt like it was a great chance to learn legal jargon and get my head around it all, but it's actually painfully tedious. I can't suggest any changes, other than a few typos, and every contract starts to look the same after a while.

I'm just another set of eyes to make sure nothing is

amiss. After that, I'll probably be sent off to do another coffee run and no doubt have to empty the dishwasher and clean the conference room after the meeting is over.

I want to be in that meeting, dammit!

I really need them to see me as more than just some pathetic assistant. I'm after responsibility, a chance to use my initiative. And the only way I'm going to get that is by doing my time. Yes, it sucks, but it's all good practice for where I want to go. If I can work my way up in this company, the world will be my oyster. That's what Ryan assured me, and I have to believe him. I've already given these guys over a year of my life on pretty pathetic pay. But I've been promised at the end of my second year that there'll be a promotion in the works, and then I can finally start becoming the sports agent I always wanted to be.

Maybe I'll even get back to those dreams I had in college. I snicker at my naivete and try to tamp down those lofty goals. It's so easy to dream when you're a student. The whole world is ahead of you, and you believe that anything is possible.

Then reality hits you like a Mack truck once you graduate and you realize that your sweet little internship won't be enough to get you where you want to go.

Reality is so much harsher than I thought it'd be. But I'm going to get there. Sometimes you just have to pay the piper to get what you want.

Focusing back on the game, I watch the players whip

across the ice and nearly jump out of my skin when someone touches my shoulder.

"Shit!" I drop my phone, and it clatters onto my desk as I whip a look over my shoulder.

"I'm sorry. Am I keeping you from the game?" Ryan narrows his eyes at me and I quickly sit up in my seat, tapping the contract and shaking my head.

"Nope. I'm nearly done here."

"I should think so." He winks at me, his smile cheesy and annoying. "Hey, after this, I want you to head out for a coffee run, and Sean needs his dry cleaning picked up." He drops the stub on my desk. "Then when you get back, you're all mine. We'll spend the afternoon going through next week's schedule, and then I need you to join me for drinks at Ryerson's Hotel so you can take some photos for social media. I've invited some of our clients along, plus a few guys from that new sports label—Heracles. I want to feel them out, see what kind of sponsorship we can pull together. It'll be mutually beneficial to get our athletes in their gear, so my demands will be high. If our guys are wearing their stuff, it'll be good for business, right?" He smooths back his slick hair, and my insides roil.

"I can't tonight, sorry. My husband is due home, and we're having dinner together."

"Not tonight." He shakes his head.

My insides pinch with annoyance. "Yes, tonight. I haven't seen him in a week." His smile drops, and I take on his blue glare with one of my own. "You told me I could have this weekend."

"But I need ya."

"Anyone can take a photo." My voice is getting weaker as my argument starts to flail. He could fire me on a whim. He may not be the big boss in this place, but he's the guy holding my puppet strings, and it won't take much for him to snip, snip, snip.

Sean will always side with Ryan because they go way back, and it's obvious he thinks the sun shines out the sleazy agent's ass. I'm pushing it by trying to argue with Ryan, and I need to shut the hell up or start packing my stuff.

He glances at my desk, eyeing the contract, then spotting my rings next to my pen holder. His lips rise into a smirk and I snatch them off the desk, shoving them on and giving him a baleful stare.

"You'll be an hour late at the most. Come with me to the hotel, snap a few photos, and then you can be on your way. I'm sure hubby won't mind." He leaves before I can argue again, and I slump back in my chair, spinning the rings around my finger and wincing when the diamond scrapes my pinkie. I pull my engagement ring off, setting it down on the desk and staring at it. My wedding band is also studded with diamonds, and last time I wore it, I ended up catching it on my favorite ribbed sweater and pulling a thread.

Closing my eyes, I pull that one off, too, and gently lay it down on top of my engagement ring. They clink together, and I'm swamped with this emotion I can't even identify. But it's not good. It's not happy, whatever the fuck it is.

Shit. Ethan's going to be so pissed. I wanted to be at home waiting for him, but it looks like I'll be walking in the door late yet again.

I grab my phone. "And fuck you very much!" I spit, dropping it back on my desk when I see the game is over and I missed the end.

Resting my head in my hands, I pull in a calming breath and feel anything but as I try to finish up the contract, then head out for the coffee run.

I'm nearly two hours late when I finally walk through the door. Ethan is waiting for me on the couch, glaring at the TV screen while he watches some inane show that I can tell he's not concentrating on.

The table is set with take-out pizza that's probably cold by now. I did try to keep him up-to-date on my movements with texts, but I admit, my last one said I'd be another thirty, and it turned into fifty-five.

"Sorry," I mutter, dumping my bag and slapping down the folder in my hands.

"More work?" he mutters.

"Just some last-minute contracts I need to read over the weekend."

Ethan tuts and shakes his head.

I clench my jaw, forcing a smile. "Welcome home."

"Thanks." His voice is gruff and sarcastic.

"I really wanted to be here when you walked in the door, but—"

"It's fine," he cuts me off.

"It's not fine. I can tell you're pissed, and I tried to get out of going to drinks with Ryan, but he—"

"Drinks, huh?" Ethan stands, shoving his hands into his hoodie pockets. He's so tall and powerful, still so damn sexy it makes my stomach quiver every single time. But his tone dampens down my desire, his arched brow and pointed look making my stomach twist in a different kind of way. "Just the two of you?"

"Of course not." I roll my eyes. "It was a bunch of people, and he wanted me to take photos."

"Selfies, no doubt," he mumbles under his breath, but I still hear him.

Snatching a cushion off the couch, I hurl it at his head. "Would you stop! There's nothing going on between me and Ryan. Ugh!" I shudder. "Even thinking that for a second is grossing me out!"

The cushion comes hurling back toward me, and I snatch it before it hits my face and biff it right back at him.

Grabbing it out of the air with a growl, he huffs at me, slapping it onto the floor with a petulant grunt.

A snort pops out of my nose before I can stop it. I'm pretty sure Billy made that exact same noise last time we were hanging with Caroline and Casey.

I fight a laugh, shaking my head. "You're being ridiculous." I point at him. "You've seen you, right? Why would I want anybody else?"

He hitches his sweats, still frowning at me like a grumpy-ass bear. "It's supposed to be our weekend. We get two days together, and then I hit the road again. And you're late, plus you've brought home a shit ton of work!"

I flick my hands wide. "What do you want me to do?"

"Quit!" he shouts.

"I can't do that." My blood starts to boil as I grit out the words. "This job is going to get me to where I want to go."

"What the fuck are you talking about? There are hundreds of sports agencies across the country."

"And this is one of the best in Colorado! And I got a job there. Do you have any idea what a huge compliment that is? I can't just turn my back on that."

"Why do you have to work for 'the best'?" He does irritating air quotes that piss me off even more. "Can't you just get a job at a smaller agency that will treat you better? The one you worked for before was great."

"They were small-time," I mutter.

"But they treated you well, and it'd give you a chance to do your law degree part-time and—"

"Would you shut up about my law degree?" I snap. "Why are you so obsessed with that?"

"Because you told me that you wanted to represent female athletes and give them the best shot, and right now you are nothing more than an unappreciated assistant at some agency that only represents men! You could be doing so much better!"

My anger flares. "I'm doing my time so that I have better opportunities later down the track! You don't know anything!" I flick my hands in the air and go to walk away, but he vaults the couch and catches my arm before I can.

"I know *you*." He stares down at me. "And you're not satisfied in this job."

I swallow, glaring up at him. "No, *you're* not satisfied that I'm not more available, and it's pissing you off."

"You're damn right I'm pissed off," he growls. "I miss you and I'm sick of seeing you so stressed out all the time. I want you to be happy. Sorry for being the worst husband of the year."

"You're not—" I let out a soft growling screech and try to wrestle myself free of his grasp, but he keeps ahold of me, dragging me closer until I'm pressed against his chest and my senses are taken over by everything that is Ethan Galloway.

He's such a presence. And my instincts immediately tune into him. I love his smell. I love his shape and texture and height and—

My brain shuts down as my body takes over. I snatch the back of his neck, yanking him toward me. His lips crush to mine as I fist the back of his hair. Slashing my tongue against his, I inhale his very essence while trying to climb up his body. Cinching me around the waist, he lifts me off the floor, and I wrap my legs around him.

He backs us against the wall, my body hitting the

solid surface and making our framed wedding photo rattle. Our chaotic kisses are turning more frenzied as he grips my thighs and then starts trailing his mouth across my jaw and down my neck.

"You're so annoying," I murmur as he sucks the sweet spot below my ear.

"You're a pain in my ass," he mumbles back, squeezing my butt and trailing hot kisses back up to my mouth. He sucks my tongue between his lips, then lightly nips my chin before swiping his tongue against mine. I groan, our argument fading to dust as I'm swept away by this tornado of want... no, need.

I *need* Ethan right now—all of him.

I need his body. I need this connection.

We obviously can't resolve our issues right now, but we can have sex.

Hot, passionate, mind-blowing sex that will cauterize our ragged wounds and take the edge off this argument we can't stop having.

Yanking at his shirt, I practically tear it off his body as he turns and drops me onto the couch. I land with a little bounce and drink him in as he pulls off his shirt in that sexy way men do—right over the top of his head. I drink in his perfect body, sitting up so I can skim my fingers down his hard ridges. His gaze is pure desire as he wriggles out of his sweats and vaults back over the couch completely naked.

His fiery look is turning me on faster than I thought possible as he kneels on the floor in front of me. I'm dripping by the time he tears my clothes off and throws them aside. Parting my legs, he flicks my feet over his shoulders and dives for my pussy.

I can't contain my cries of pleasure as he makes quick work of sending my body into a frenzy. The tip of his tongue circles my clit while he squeezes my breasts, and I fight for air.

I want to tell him how much I've missed him, but I can't form words. My body is too on fire to even make one syllable pop out.

But I have missed him. Not just his touch, his tongue, the way he can drive me to the point of insanity, but I've missed being around him, laughing with him, teasing him, snuggling with him on the couch.

We can get back to that place, right? Shit, we could snuggle right after this. Pretend our fight never happened and go back to the way things were.

I lift my head and glance down between my legs when Ethan pauses. Our eyes connect, and I'm locked in place, held still by his gaze that captured my heart all those years ago when I was just a clueless freshman and he was the guy I was trying to prank.

I miss those days. Not the whole pranking, sorority bullshit, but the stuff after that, when I lived at Hockey House and our biggest concern was making it to class on time and figuring out what to have for dinner.

My lips part, my breath catching as he glides his fingers inside me. His tongue flicks my clit, and I can't hold his gaze anymore. Tipping my head back with a moan, I grip the back of the couch and let out a reckless groan that builds to a panting scream as he works my clit, thrusts his fingers a little deeper, and sends me over the edge.

"Fuck." The word drags out of my mouth as I ride the wave, his fingers still working me as I struggle to regulate my senses. My hips jerk while I moan and pant, barely able to see straight as he climbs onto the couch with me, his fingers slowly pulling out of me and spreading my folds.

Biting my bottom lip, I hold my breath and wait for that pure moment of ecstasy. The anticipation is killing me, and I let out another raucous wail when he finally plunges into me.

"Yes, baby!" Gripping the couch, I lift my hips on his next thrust, and he grabs my ass, holding me up and rising to his knees so he can plunge into me again and again.

His thrusts are a little rough and reckless, but they're exactly what I need. He's filling me whole, disconnecting every circuit in my brain until the only ones still functioning are the pleasure sensors. They're riding high, exploding like fireworks as Ethan's ragged breaths soon match mine, his face distorting as the orgasm starts to build within him.

I can sense it coming and reach for his taut forearms, wrapping my fingers around his straining muscles as he starts to jerk, then plunges deep and hard.

His groans join mine, creating a chorus of ecstasy as

he holds me up and empties himself completely. A fine sheen of sweat coats his skin, and as he starts to relax, he lays his slick body over mine.

I cup the back of his head, running my fingers through his messy locks when he nestles his chin into the crook of my neck.

"You know you are the best husband in the world, right?"

He rests on his elbows so he can look into my eyes. The impish grin on his face is adorable, and I touch his chin, smiling when he replies, "Love you, lil' mouse."

And those are the words ringing in my head as we drift off to sleep, still naked and wrapped in each other's arms.

I wake around three in the morning, my mind alert as work worries filter into my brain. I need to get these contracts done before Ryan texts me in the morning to check that they are.

Ethan is still out for the count, and there's no point in me lying here awake and worried when I could be using this time to get shit done.

I slip off the couch, careful not to disturb him. Grabbing the first shirt I can find, I slip it over my head and smile at the way Ethan's clothes always dwarf me.

Grabbing that stack of contracts, I figure I can proof them by flashlight. That way, by the time Ethan wakes up, I'll be free for the rest of the weekend... hopefully. If I don't get any work calls to disturb me.

Flicking on my phone light, I start reading documents

and don't notice Ethan wake until he moves on the couch. His dark shadow looms, and I lift my light, checking his face with a grin.

But all I can see is a dejected frown.

He stands there before me in all his naked glory, and that awesome moment we shared on the couch turns to dust as he glances at me doing paperwork, then shuffles past the table. "I'm going to bed."

His footsteps retreating up to our loft room say the rest for him.

You left me after we had epic sex.

You're putting work above me yet again.

I close my eyes, swearing under my breath and trying to negotiate how to figure out this shit show.

I'm trying so fucking hard to make everything work and failing around every corner. I can't help wondering if something is about to break...

I glance at the dark stairwell, a shudder running through me because I'm terrified that it might be the one thing that's most important to me.

MAY

CHAPTER 10
CAROLINE

Tammy and Baxter's wedding is just over a month away, and I'm feeling like a whale already. I have no idea what I'm going to wear to the event... or if I even want to go.

Of course you want to go!

But Rachel will be there, and I don't want things to be awkward. I'm already starting to waddle, and the thought of trying to dress up nice for a wedding with this big belly...

You were bigger than this when you and Casey got married.

Ugh, I so don't need a lecture from my brain right now.

I'm hot and tired and flustered.

The boys have been dynamite today. Thankfully, Troy is napping right now and Billy is quietly playing downstairs. When Troy first went down for his nap, Billy decided that playing drums on the pots would be a great idea, but I put a quick stop to that. Thank *everything* he didn't wake his little brother and I've had a small reprieve this afternoon. I even let Billy watch TV, but he only lasted about thirty minutes before getting bored, so I should really go down and check on him.

I have my fingers crossed that he's building a race-track or fire station with his blocks.

"Please let that be true," I whisper, tears suddenly burning my eyes.

I have no idea what's got me so emotional today, but I seem to be tearing up at the drop of a hat.

Because you want to go to Casey's game and you can't.

I'll be lucky if the boys will give me a chance to watch it on TV. The house is always chaos around dinner/bath time, and there's no way I'll get to keep an eye on the game. I'm gutted. Casey's been having the best season, and his team made it all the way through to the second round of the Stanley Cup playoffs. They're losing the series three to one, so there's a chance this is his last game of the season, and I desperately want to go and support him, but my parents are out of town and Jolie, who was all lined up to babysit, bailed this morning. It was a work emergency, so I couldn't be mad at her, but still...

Totally bummed out.

I would ask the neighbor, but Mrs. Mattley is getting on now, and I only ever ask her to babysit once the boys are already settled for the night.

There's no way I'll make the game, and I just have to get over my disappointment and be okay with it. I'll leave the TV on so that anytime I walk through the living room, I can catch a glimpse of the action. I might even see if Billy can play "Spot Daddy" for a minute.

My phone starts ringing and I slip it out of my pocket, a smile tugging at my lips when I see who's calling.

"Hey, Lani."

"Ugh, you're not going to believe it!"

I pick Billy's dirty sweater off the floor and dump it into the hamper. "Asher thwarted your proposal plan again, huh?"

"How does he keep doing this to me? I had it all lined up. I'd arrange for him to pick me up from school, and he was going to walk into my classroom and the students were going to throw balloons in the air while I got down on one knee. They were primed and pumped and—"

"What happened?"

"He just waited for me in his car and refused to come in even when I lied and told him I needed help carrying stuff!"

I can't help a soft giggle. "He seriously didn't offer to help you? That's so unlike him."

"I know!" Lani huffs. "He told me one of my students could help me, which means he knows I was planning on popping the question."

"Uh-huh." I nod, padding down the hallway to check on Billy.

"It's just payback for last month when he tried to propose and I made sure I 'got lost' and couldn't find the restaurant."

"You two are unbelievable." I shake my head. "You've turned this into a huge competition and taken all the romance out of it."

"I can't let him win, Caroline." She sounds incredulous.

I roll my eyes and push open the playroom door, my eyebrows dipping when I notice that Billy's not in here anymore.

Oh shit.

With a jerk, I spin, Lani's complaints turning to white noise as I realize I just made a rookie mistake in the parenting department. Things are too quiet! I left it too long to check on him, and now Billy will be up to some kind of mischief in the house and I'll—

I race down the stairs, veering into the kitchen and screeching to a stop in the doorway. My heart plummets into my bare feet as I take in the mess.

"Billy," I whine, unable to help myself.

"Hi, Mommy. I'm baking!" He throws his hands in the air, releasing a cloud of flour. It wafts through the air before landing on all the surfaces, which are already coated in a layer of white dust. Even Fezzik's a little snow dog right now, his fur caked in white paste.

"Did you wash the dog, then flour him?"

"Uh-huh!" He smiles brightly. "He kept shaking, and the flour came off. Water helps it stick better."

I frown at him, willing my voice to stay calm as I grit out, "You know you're not supposed to bake without Mommy."

His big blue eyes go a little larger, and he gives me this adorably coy smile. "Wanted it to be a surpwise."

"Oh, it's a surprise."

"What's going on?" Lani's voice finally registers in my ear.

I let out a sharp breath. "Billy decided that baking would be a great idea, and my kitchen is now covered in flour and..." I creep around the counter and wince, noting the powdered sugar that's been dropped all over the floor, and Billy's pants and... "Oh crap."

"Oh crap!" Billy yells, punching his little fists in the air.

"Billy!" I growl. "You know that's a bad word."

"Sorry, Mommy."

"You got into the food coloring? How did you even reach it?"

"I climbed." His expression is so sweet, his explanation so simple, and all I can feel is a cold shudder as I picture Billy climbing up the pantry shelves to the very top and then tumbling onto the floor and hurting himself.

Closing my eyes, I suck in a breath, fighting for calm, but I'm a trembling mess when my eyes pop back open and I stare at the bright red and blue droplets dripping off the bench, landing on my beautiful white drawers and handles, dripping down my cupboards like neon tears.

I can't help sniffing, tears building quickly as I contemplate the epic cleanup.

"How can one kid create so much mess in such a short period of time?"

"I'm sorry, sweetie." Lani's voice is soft with sympathy, but I'm sure she's also fighting laughter. "I wish I lived closer so I could come and help you."

"Me too," I murmur, feeling so alone right now that I want to curl into a ball and cry.

But there's no time for that, because Troy's cries come through the baby monitor perched on the kitchen counter.

"Troy's awake!" Billy gasps with excitement, jumping down off his stool and running for the stairs. Fezzik barks and goes to chase him.

"Wait!" I quickly stop them both, grabbing the back of Billy's shirt and sticking out my foot to avert Fezzik. He rears for the doggy door as I give him a sharp "Fezzik, outside! Now!" Dragging Billy back toward me, I quickly warn him, "Don't you walk your messy self through this house. You need to get in the shower, right now."

"But I wanna see Troy!" He stamps his foot, flour puffing up from the floor as his bottom lip pulls into a pout.

Troy cries a little louder, and then the doorbell rings.

Are you fucking kidding me?

I glance toward the entryway at the same time Billy does, and before I can snatch him, he takes off running to the front door.

"Lani, I gotta go," I rush out, hanging up on my best friend, then bolting after my little wild child and reaching the door just as he pulls it open to reveal the last person I thought would be visiting us.

CHAPTER 11
RACHEL

"Hi." I wave, taking in Billy's sweet expression and Caroline's flustered frown. Her red curls are pulled back into a messy bun, and tendrils are falling around her flushed cheeks. Billy is coated in flour and powdered sugar, his fingers stained pink and blue—I assume that's food coloring—and Troy is crying somewhere in the house.

Caroline holds the edge of the door, gaping at me and Liam. Tears are filling her eyes, and even though I thought I couldn't handle seeing her until after her baby was born, I end up stepping through the door and wrapping her in a hug.

"What do you need us to do?" I ask.

She sniffs and clings to me, her fingers digging into my shoulders as she whimpers, "I've gotta go get Troy, but if you could maybe help me with the kitchen..."

"On it." Liam scoops Billy into his arms. "C'mere, you little mess."

"Uncle Liam." Billy giggles and screeches when he starts getting tickled by my gorgeous husband. He's going to make the best dad.

A thrill whistles through me as I let Caroline go so she can get Troy from his crib.

She darts away, and I glance into the living room, surveying the riotous mess—books all over the floor, a minefield of toys, cushions strewn everywhere, plastic plates with half-eaten snacks on the kiddy table, and a mug of what looks like stone-cold coffee sitting on the window ledge. I walk in and start gathering up the plates and mug, walking them through to the kitchen, where I'm met with quite the mess.

"Oh boy," I whisper.

"I know, right?" Liam laughs and shakes his head, dusting flour and powdered sugar off his shirt. "Lucky I always have a spare change of clothes in the car." Billy laughs and slaps his flour-coated hands on Liam's shirt, giggling at the horrified look on his uncle's face. "Oi, you." He growls and Billy squeals, ready to take off running, but Liam snatches him before he can. "No way, *papi*. You're helping me clean up. Where does Mommy keep the broom?"

Billy blinks up at him, then starts walking for the laundry room. I set the dishes in the sink and look at the mess, wondering where to even start.

Poor Caroline. Looks like she's having a rough day.

I'm glad we stopped by. We hadn't actually planned on it. We're just in Denver for Casey and Ethan's game tonight. It could be their last of the season, and we wanted to be there to show our support.

We were a little early, and Liam suggested we swing past Caroline's place and tell her the good news.

"You up for seeing her?" He glanced at me, his expression so kind that I felt my heart swell like it always does. "If it's still too much, we can leave it."

"No, it's a good idea." I smiled. "We're gonna be parents now, and it'll be nice to tell her in person."

Excitement pulsed between us, and I couldn't help laughing.

Ahhh! I'm going to be a mama!

That burst of pleasure explodes in my chest again, and I bite my bottom lip. We got the call a few nights ago. It's miraculous, because adoption takes a long time. We'd been warned that it would take months for everything to go through, but then it happened.

A teenage mother in Boulder is looking for a young couple to adopt her baby. We're due to meet with her on Tuesday, and I'm so excited I can hardly stand it. I know I shouldn't get ahead of myself, but the adoption agency were so positive when we spoke with them on the phone.

"You two will be perfect, and the mother really likes you. We'll set the meeting up and go from there. I know I can't promise anything, but this is looking really good." She was thrilled for us.

I'm thrilled for us. This is happening so much faster

than I thought it would, and I'm giddy. The day she called, I popped out and bought a couple of small outfits. I couldn't help myself. Liam and I are getting a newborn. That little girl is going to be ours right from the outset, and it'll be amazing.

I can't wait to tell Caroline that we'll be raising daughters together. Our babies will only be a few months apart.

Billy walks back in with a kid-sized broom while Liam trails him with a bucket and mop.

"We'll start with the countertops," Liam tells him. "Let's brush all of this off onto the floor, and then we can clean that up, okay?"

Billy nods, his enthusiasm waning as he looks at the huge mess he made.

"You made it, kid. You gotta clean it up." Liam winks at him. "Come on, it'll be fun."

With a little frown, the three-year-old takes the cloth I just wet for him and starts wildly wiping the counter. I laugh and stop him, showing him how to do it properly. He's pretty good at copying me, so when Troy's cries come out of the baby monitor, I offer to go and check if Caroline needs my help.

"Okay." Liam brushes his lips across mine just before I walk out of the room.

I smile, the simple gesture making my lips tingle. I love my husband so damn much. And I'm going to love him even more watching him raise our daughter.

"Caroline?" I softly call when I reach the top of the stairs.

"In here." She sounds out of sorts, and when I step into the room and get a whiff of what just came out of Troy, I understand why.

"Wow." I pinch my nose.

"I know, right?" Caroline blows a curl off her cheek. "He's definitely Casey's kid!" She gags, pulling a face that makes Troy giggle, while wrapping up the diaper and shoving it into the bin.

She doesn't laugh along with her son, and I feel sad that she's having such a bad day. It's obviously gotten the better of her, and I think I get it. Kids can be hard work. But she's got babies to love and cherish. Isn't that the best thing in the world?

I clamp my lips against saying that to her, smiling down at Troy and drawing circles on his tummy while Caroline gets out a fresh change of clothes for him.

She starts wrestling them onto his squirming body, and I can't help laughing at Troy's sweet smile.

"You are too cute, little one."

His smile grows, drool dropping off his lower lip. Caroline catches it with a cloth and shakes her head. "These fresh clothes will be dirty in five minutes, I guarantee it."

"You must be doing laundry constantly." I laugh.

"Yep, my washer and dryer get a workout, that's for sure."

She picks Troy up, standing him on the changing table. He stamps his little feet and bobs up and down, making it hard to pull his pants up. Finally, he's good to go, and she perches him on her hip, his little leg curling around her extended belly. "So…" She looks at me. "It's nice to see you. How've you been?"

"Yeah, good." I look at her, then glance away with a soft cringe. "I'm sorry I haven't been able to see you."

"I get it." She nods. "Really." Squeezing my shoulder lightly, she gathers up Troy's dirty clothes and pops them into the hamper.

"I hear you're having a girl. Congratulations. You must be over the moon."

"Yeah, it's exciting." Caroline sounds anything but excited. She winces as Troy grabs a handful of her hair and gives it a tug. "Ouch."

He laughs like it's funny, and she takes his hand, detangling his fingers from her hair. Her messy bun is now total chaos, clumps of hair sticking out on the side. I can tell it's taking major effort for her to stay calm. Her eyes are glistening as she tries to smooth her hair back. Troy is bobbing on her hip, wiping his drool across her shoulder before squealing right in her ear. Popping him onto the floor, she rubs the top of his head before he toddles across the room toward me.

I crouch down to greet him while Caroline frowns, retying her hair and trying to wipe Troy's drool and snot off her shirt. She gives up, rolling her eyes and shaking her head.

"I better go check out the kitchen." She sighs.

"It's okay. You can relax. Liam and Billy are on

cleaning detail, and they're doing a wonderful job." I smile, and she blinks in surprise.

"Billy's cleaning?"

"He is." I nod with a grin.

Caroline's shoulders relax a little, and she manages a fleeting smile. "So, Lani tells me you're looking into adoption." She crosses her arms over her beach-ball stomach, trying to look bright and cheerful, but her poor, tired face can barely muster it.

News always travels fast in our group, which is why we haven't told anyone yet that we're getting a baby. We want to meet the mother first and get the paperwork all signed. But maybe it'll be okay to share this with Caroline. It'll be a happy distraction for her. We can celebrate raising our daughters together. Mine will be born only three months after hers.

It's impossible to fight my grin as I say, "Actually—" My phone rings before I can spill the beans. "Sorry," I murmur, pulling it out of my pocket and checking the screen.

My heart jumps with a little skip as I see it's from the adoption agency, and I answer with a broad grin. "Hello."

"Hi, Rachel." The second I hear her voice, I know it's not good. Her tone is too flat.

My smile disappears, heat spreading through me as she sighs and punches me right through the heart.

"I hate to be making this call. I really thought it was a sure thing. She seemed adamant that she wanted to put her baby up for adoption. Everything was lined up, but...

I just got a call from her parents. They've decided to keep the baby."

I don't know what to say, so I just stand there quietly while she tries to encourage me and tell me this isn't the end. There'll be another baby out there who needs a home and—

"How long will that take?" I interrupt her.

"I can't say for sure. Sometimes it's only a matter of weeks; other times it can take months, even years. But you're in our system now, and we'll contact you as soon as we find a good match. In the meantime, you could always consider foster care."

I close my eyes. The thought of caring for children only to have to give them away again sends a searing pain through me. I don't think I'm cut out for that. I wish I could be. It's such an admirable thing to do, but I know myself well enough... and I can't do foster care. My heart will break every time a child is sent back to their parents or moved on somewhere else.

I just want a baby who can be mine... a child Liam and I can raise. I want a family that I can watch grow.

"Have a think on it," she murmurs, obviously sensing my distress. "Once again, I'm sorry. I'll be in touch."

She mercifully ends the call, and I pull the phone away from my ear.

"Everything okay?" Caroline steps toward me and I back away, forcing myself to nod and smile.

"Yeah. It's fine."

"You don't look—"

"I'm fine." I brighten my smile, my insides trembling with the effort of keeping it together.

Caroline definitely doesn't believe me, but she quickly gets distracted when Troy starts giggling, and we both glance down to see him gleefully pulling wet wipes out of the container and throwing them over his shoulder.

"Troy, stop." Caroline crouches down, tutting as she takes the container and then starts picking up the wet wipes. "Honestly, this day is a nightmare."

"Yeah, such a nightmare," I mutter. I can't help it.

Standing there with her pregnant belly and a beautiful baby boy at her feet... what the fuck does she have to complain about?

Troy lets out a squelchy fart, which stinks to high heaven, and Caroline sighs, letting out a whimper as she lifts him up and checks his diaper.

"Again? I just changed you."

Troy giggles and she huffs, laying him back down and grumbling about endless diapers and stinky poop and...

And I lose it.

"Do you have any idea how lucky you are?" I snap.

Caroline and Troy both jerk, twisting their heads to gape at me. Troy blinks his big eyes, and Caroline's lips part.

"Don't you dare complain about one. Single. Thing!" I point at her. "Your life is perfect, okay? You have two beautiful boys and a daughter on the way! How dare you stand there whining when there are some people out there who would kill to have what you have."

"Ray, I—"

"Don't even talk to me," I screech. "I can't be here. I can't watch this!" A sob pops out of my mouth and I spin from the room, racing down the stairs as Caroline feebly tries to call me back.

I ignore her, storming out to the car and slamming myself into it.

Covering my face, I give in to my tears and let them wrench through my body. My stomach convulses, my shoulders shaking as I sit in the Pierce driveway and mourn once again.

But this time it's worse, because I'm not just lamenting the loss of this little girl who I thought would be ours. I'm also riddled with guilt over shouting in front of Troy and being such a bitch to Caroline. Her day has been bad enough as it is, and I've probably made it a hundred times worse. But I can't walk back into that house.

I can't do it.

I just want to go.

"Hurry up, Liam," I whisper, cringing when I think about what Caroline must be saying to him.

Swiping tears off my face, I sniff and start hunting for a tissue. I find one at the very bottom of my bag and whimper, ripping it as I pull it from the packet, then weeping all over again.

Seriously, Ray? You're crying over a ripped tissue.

That gets the tears going even more, and by the time Liam finally joins me, my face is a blotchy mess.

"Sorry I took a minute," he murmurs as soon as he slips into the driver's seat. "I wanted to split myself in half and be in two places at once. I couldn't just leave Billy and—"

"It's okay." I shake my head, wiping my face again and sniffing. "You did the right thing. I'm the one being unreasonable."

"Cariño," he whispers, lightly cupping the back of my head. "It's okay. Caroline said you got a phone call."

"Yeah," I squeak. "From the adoption agency."

He sighs, sadness washing over his expression as he reads my face and immediately works out the news.

"I should have known it was too good to be true. We were warned this whole process would take months, a year even, and it all came together so quickly." I shake my head, the words wobbling out of me.

"Is she keeping it?" His voice is rough and gravelly, like it's hurting him to speak.

"Yeah." My stomach jerks with a sob. "The family wants to keep it. Her parents called and said the adoption's not happening anymore," I whimper. "I'm heartbroken."

"Me too." He nods, his lips rising into a brave smile, but it's etched with sadness, and he's soon frowning down at his lap.

I lean toward him, wrapping my arms around his neck, and he holds me tight. "This sucks."

"Yeah." He squeezes me close and I instantly feel better, knowing I'm not alone in this pain. "But we'll get through this, and when the time's right, we'll get our baby."

"You don't know that." My words are muffled by his shirt.

He strokes my hair. "I guess not." Then he pulls back to cup my face. His soft brown gaze is so deep and beautiful. I sink into it. "We have each other. And Ray, that might have to be enough."

My lips tremble as fresh tears line my lashes.

His eyebrows crinkle with worry. "Is it enough for you?"

"Of course it is." I nod. "I love you. You're the best husband in the world. And I'm grateful, I really am. I just wanted the whole package, you know? Does that make me a bad person?"

"No." A tender smile spreads across his face. "You've got a mother's heart. And I don't believe your desire to have kids would be so damn strong if we weren't meant to have them." He brushes his thumb across my cheek. "The right baby is going to come along at the right time. We have to believe that."

The hope and conviction in his eyes are beautiful, and I wish I could be strong like him. I wish I had his faith. Launching back into his arms, I cling to him, praying that his hope is enough for both of us.

CHAPTER 12
CASEY

I hold my breath, my heart racing as my team heads for the goal. Ethan's stick work is fucking awesome.

"Go, man! Go!" I shout, slapping my gloved hands on the boards as he approaches the goal.

The crowd is going wild, the rising cheer around us near deafening, but I love it.

Shit, I wish Caroline could be here. I was so gutted when she texted to tell me how all of the plans had fallen through. I wanted to call her and make sure she was okay, but it was too close to game time, and I didn't get a chance.

I hope she's managing to watch this.

Ethan flicks off the pass, skating around a defender and setting up for a perfect goal.

This is it. We're going to tie the game and—

The goalie does the splits, and moving like lightning,

he flicks his leg out and stops the puck before it can fire into the net. My heart deflates, because two seconds later, the end-of-game buzzer goes.

"Shit," I mutter. We're out.

It's been a great season, and to get to round two of the Stanley Cup playoffs is epic, but it's not our year.

"Next time," the guy beside me murmurs as we watch the other team celebrate, huddling in the middle of the rink while our players skate off the ice.

The mood is a little somber as we head for the lockers, but Coach gives us a pretty rousing speech.

"I'm proud of you guys. We've had a great season. And we're going to play even better next time around. You're a solid team, so you hold your heads high and celebrate the year we've had together."

We let out a few whoops and cheers, the mood rising as we process our loss and start to look forward to some much-needed time off. There'll still be training and fitness and a myriad of other things to keep us conditioned, but we won't be traveling for away games, and I'll get to spend some decent time with my family.

Bring it the fuck on.

An ache to see them travels through me, but I can't head home just yet.

A bunch of our friends traveled down from Nolan to watch us play, and I need to go hang with them for a little minute.

Ethan and I meet up with them outside the arena. I get a monster hug from Kai, and he starts a playful tussle, his scrawny arms taking me on. His laughter is adorable, and I pick him up, throwing him over my shoulder with a roar that quickly dies in my throat. The look on Ethan's face is blacker than ink. Damn, he's in a foul mood tonight, and he's gonna kill this party if we don't deal immediately.

At first, I think he's struggling with the loss, maybe overanalyzing that last pass and wondering what he could have done better.

I lower Kai to the ground, about to tell my teammate that he set his final attempt at goal up perfectly, when I realize he's not pissed about that. As Kai settles in beside Baxter, I finally notice...

Mick's not waiting with our group.

I glance around, silently asking where she is, and Ethan mutters darkly, "Work thing. She got a phone call just before the game and left."

With a soft hiss, I pat him on the shoulder, and he stalks ahead, striding along beside Liam, who's looking a little on the sad side as well. His arm is around Rachel's waist, and she's looking morose too.

What the fuck is going on with everyone tonight?

Sure, we lost, but we're hitting our summer vacation: next month we'll be celebrating Baxter and Tammy's wedding, and the month after that, we'll be welcoming a new baby girl into the world.

Holy shit, I'm having a daughter.

A thrill whistles through me. It's tender and sweet and protective. The idea of holding that little girl in my arms... shit, I'm gonna look after her with everything I've got. My little angel. I can't wait to meet her.

It makes me want to ditch these guys and get home to my woman. I need to hold her, kiss her, celebrate my season with her. It's so wrong that she couldn't be here tonight.

Her day turned into such a shit show.

Pulling my phone out of my bag, I notice I missed a call from her and lift the phone to my ear. There's a voice message waiting for me.

"Hey, babe." She sniffs, her voice wobbling. "I just wanted to wish you well for the game. You're probably already set, maybe even on the ice right now." She squeaks and my eyebrows pucker, because fuck, she's crying. "I really wanted to be there to support you, but my day has just gone from bad to worse. I don't want to burden you with it, but I'd like to resign from parenting, please. I'm handing in my notice." I snicker and shake my head. "And if you could please whisk me away to some tropical island where all I have to think about is what cocktail to order while I lounge on a chair and not have to answer questions or clean up poop or get yelled at..." She sucks in a breath, her voice going squeaky again. "That'd be great."

And her tears start in earnest. She blubbers a good-bye, and then I hear Billy shouting something before the line goes dead.

My heart squeezes into a painful ball as I immediately call her back... although she would have left this message a few hours ago. Hopefully by now the boys are in bed, asleep, and she's feeling a little better, but still... I wasn't there for her when she needed me.

Fuck.

I'm so glad the season's over.

She doesn't answer the call, and as much as I want to hang with my friends, I need to get home to my wife.

"Guys, I gotta bail," I tell them before we even reach the restaurant we planned on hanging in.

They all spin to face me.

"Everything okay?" Baxter asks, while Kai's little face drops with disappointment. I feel kind of bad about that, but...

"Yeah." I hold up my phone with a frown. "Sounds like Caroline's had a shitty day, so I'm gonna... go." My words slow as I notice Rachel's expression pinch, her skin paling as she glances to the ground.

Liam pulls her close, murmuring something against her ear before kissing her, then flashing me a closed-mouth smile, which I don't believe.

What the fuck is going on?

I nearly ask him, but I want to get home, so I do a quick round of goodbyes and run for my truck. Shit, it's going to be a fucking morose "party" for those guys tonight. With Ethan's foul mood and whatever the hell is bothering Rachel and Liam... all I can say is poor Baxter and Kai.

My insides skitter as I wonder what awaits me.

I call again, but Caroline's still not answering. It

makes me drive a little faster, and I'm soon turning onto our street. The lights are off downstairs, which means everyone is settled for the night. Maybe she's not answering my calls because she's asleep. If it's been a crap-fest of a day, Caroline might have hit the pillow as soon as the boys were down. As much as she wants to resign her position as mother, I know she never would. She only says shit like that to me in jest and on the really tough days.

Shit. It's been a long season for her this year. Pregnancy is hard enough on the body without having to look after two energetic toddlers. I'm glad I'm going to be around more to support her.

Closing the front door as quietly as I can, I dump my stuff, then flick off the porch light she always leaves on for me and make my way upstairs. Fezzik meets me at the top of the stairs, his tail wagging.

"Hey, buddy." I pet his head, then lead him back into the boys' room.

He jumps onto the end of Billy's bed—his favorite spot—curling into a little ball at his feet. I creep in, the night-light casting a soft glow across my kids' faces. They're both out for the count, Billy starfishing it while Troy is curled on his side, hugging his blanket and looking damn adorable.

I lightly brush my fingers over his strawberry blond curls, then give Billy a little peck on the forehead before sneaking out to find my wife.

Steam is billowing out from our en suite bathroom,

and I now know why she wasn't answering my calls. It was shower time, and she must have had a nice, long one. Good. I hope it's relaxed her a bit.

Padding across the room, I gently push the door open and find her wrapped in a towel that's barely covering her perfect ass. I can see the round curve of her cheek as she bends over. Her leg is perched on the edge of the bathtub while she awkwardly tries to shave her legs. Her big belly keeps getting in the way, and she tuts, adjusting herself and trying to reach a spot by her ankle.

"Hey, sexy." My voice is a husky rumble, and she glances over her shoulder. Her red hair is up in a messy top knot, curls splashing down around her face, and I swear she's never looked more beautiful.

"Hey, you."

"Need a hand?"

She grunts, and I'm sure she's about to refuse me, but then she holds out the razor. "Can you just check if I've missed any spots?"

"Sure." I grin, eyeing her with hungry desire as I step into the bathroom.

Shit, she's fucking fire. Her tits have swollen from the pregnancy, and she's got this glow about her, which is a complete turn-on.

I wet the razor and crouch down, gently catching all the places she missed.

"You know you don't have to shave your legs for me. I know it's awkward for you right now."

She harrumphs. "I don't shave my legs for *you*. I shave

them for me. I like how smooth they are when I'm done. It makes me feel pretty."

"You'd still be pretty with hairy legs."

She rolls her eyes. "I feel prettier with them shaved, so I don't care how monstrously huge I get, I'm still shaving my damn legs."

I laugh and kiss her knee, finishing off the other leg before dropping the razor into the sink. She starts to rinse everything off and I stand behind her, gliding my fingers up her bare legs and nibbling her shoulder.

"What is that look on your face, Mr. Pierce?" She's gazing at me in the mirror, and I catch her eye, my grin hiding none of my desire as I grab the back of her towel and yank it off.

She gives a little gasp, then laughs as I flick the towel over my shoulder and admire her stunning tits in the bathroom mirror. Cupping my hands beneath them, I give those luscious funbags a gentle squeeze, lightly pinching her nipples as I nestle my body behind hers. I'm hard already, and I can tell by the gleam in her eyes and the way she nudges her ass back against me that she can feel my desire.

"Damn, you're looking sexy tonight, Cherry Girl."

She shakes her head.

"Baby, you're always sexy to me." My hands round her distended belly. She's got stretch marks even though she's religious with the moisturizer. I know she hates them, but they do nothing to scar her beauty. They're part of her, and I love them because of that. They're marks that represent what an amazing woman she is. She's grown three babies already. Three. And she's birthed two of them, which is fucking epic.

This woman in my arms is amazing. And so fucking sexy.

My dick grows even harder, straining against my pants as I grind against her perfect ass.

She groans, dipping her head forward and closing her eyes.

For a second, I think she's about to tell me she doesn't want this. Maybe she needs to talk about her shitty day first. Maybe she's too stressed out to really let go and enjoy this with me. As disappointing as that is, I'll accept it.

But when I go to step away, her hips thrust back again —her silent show of permission—and all I can whisper is "That's my girl."

Her lips twitch with a grin as she catches my eye in the mirror before bending her head back so she can kiss me. I glide my tongue along her lips, my hands trailing from her stomach to her thighs before cresting up her hips and then gliding north to play with her nipples.

She moans again, and I love how I know every one of her sweet sounds now. She can tell me without a word exactly what she wants, and I happily deliver, pinching her hardened nipples and sucking her neck.

Reaching back, she threads her fingers into my hair, closing her eyes and tipping her head back with another groan. She wants more, so I glide my hands back down, rounding my fingers over her ass and playing with her pussy from behind.

Her breath hitches as I dip my middle finger between her folds and start stroking her inner walls. I love this warm oasis, have studied it in depth, and enjoy the sweet gasp that pops out of her as I find her G-spot and give it a tickle.

My dick is straining to get free.

All in good time, my friend. Let's make her come first.

I glide another finger inside her, stretching, reveling in the wet eagerness that greets me as I plunge a little deeper, then pull my fingers back, teasing her sweet spot until she's gasping and leaning forward to grip the bench. She pants over the sink, and I hope she doesn't come too quickly, because I want to keep going with this thing.

Sliding open the bathroom drawer, I keep stroking her inner walls while scrambling for her vibrator. It's bright pink and easy to find. Her gaze darts to mine in the mirror, her lips rising in a playful smirk as I switch it on and a low hum reverberates around the room.

"You're going to try and kill me with multiple orgasms, aren't you?"

Her face is fucking beautiful, her expression puckering in ecstasy as I lay the vibrator against her clit. Her lips pop open with a silent scream, and I rub my scruffy whiskers across her shoulders, murmuring between kisses, "It wouldn't be a bad way to go, baby."

I glide my fingers out of her pussy and let her sink against the vibrator for a moment, supporting her belly while she bends her knees and loses herself. Her head tips forward, and the sounds coming out of her are magic.

I love her pleasure.

I love watching her fall apart.

It's so fucking hot, and I can't wait to plunge my cock inside her.

But first...

Trailing my fingers back around her body, I wait until she's close to the edge, then help her take a flying leap by thrusting two fingers back inside her and curling them against her G-spot.

"Ahhh," she groans. "Yes. Baby, yes!" Her sounds turn to high-pitched squeaks, and I know she's about to shatter.

I watch in wonder, loving the way her muscles go taut just before the explosion. Then she's vibrating, squirming on her toes and shuddering as the orgasm washes through her. She's still riding out the wave when I set the vibrator aside and softly murmur, "You want more?"

I'm already unzipping my pants, grinning when she nods and pants, "Hell yes, baby."

Mr. Jones is more than happy to come out and play. He pops free as I shove my pants down, looking for release. The second my tip hits her entrance, he's doing a happy dance. I can feel his glee as I grasp Caroline's hips and thrust into her.

She cries out the way she always does, and I revel in that sound... revel in that feeling of being wrapped in her warm center. She's fucking fantastic, and I pump into her, closing my eyes and absorbing every sensation traveling through me.

"Fuck yeah, baby. You're so hot."

She whimpers, thrusting back against me and bending forward for a different angle. I deliver, my pace picking up as I pound into her the way she likes—hard and fast.

I grip her ass cheeks, giving them a firm squeeze and loving the way pregnancy softens her curves, giving me more to hold on to. I love the way her body has changed over the years, enjoying her at every stage, falling deeper and deeper as we grow together.

Yeah, that's a fucking philosophical thing to think when my cock is buried in her pussy, but it's true. The longer I'm with this woman, the more I love her. She's become a part of my soul.

She whimpers again, gripping the edge of the vanity and nudging back, telling me to go a little faster, plunge a little deeper. I happily oblige, breaths punching out of me faster and faster as my body starts to reach that point of mind-blowing ecstasy.

"Fuck, you feel good, baby."

"You too," she pants, tipping her head back and moaning some more.

I slow my pace, wanting to draw this out, because being inside her is so fucking good and these chances are getting harder to find. The boys are asleep, and I need to take advantage of this downtime we've got together.

Gliding my hands in front of her, I slow my pace to these long, languid pulls as my fingers find her clit.

"You *are* trying to kill me," she whispers. "Death by multiple orgasms."

I grin, catching her eye in the mirror. "Like I said, it's a good way to go, baby."

"Yeah." She smiles back at me, her eyes bright and stunning before she snaps them shut, her lips parting as I hit her sweet spot again. She burrows farther back into me, my cock starting to twitch as her inner walls clamp around me.

"Keep going," she squeaks. "I need that friction."

I start pumping a little faster, and she lets out these gasping screams, her hand clamping over mine when she hits another orgasm and starts milking my cock. It takes me all of five seconds to start jerking inside her, the climax hitting me like a wrecking ball. I slam into her, uncontrolled thrusts that make us both cry out while I empty myself.

At least I can't get her pregnant again right now, right?

Shit, she says my sperm must burn through the condoms, and it's no wonder why. They probably fire through those things because she turns me on so fucking hard. She makes me come like a nuclear explosion because she's so fucking hot. Her pussy is still clenching around me, making it hard to breathe or do anything but clutch her hips and hold on.

My strangled cries are no doubt comical as my body tries to regulate again.

It's taking its sweet time, and I jerk once more before finally finding my breath again. My heart rate slowly starts to decelerate. I stay inside her, resting my forehead against her shoulder, then lightly kissing a path up her neck as I hum the chorus to "Sweet Caroline."

She lets out a throaty laugh, biting her bottom lip and staring at me in the mirror.

Her blue eyes are bright, smiling at me before her lips follow suit.

"Love you, Cherry Girl," I whisper.

"I love you too."

Her gaze turns misty, but I'm pretty sure these are happy tears.

Pregnancy has always made her emotional, and I've had to harden myself, as her tears have always killed me in the past. But I'm adjusting... mostly.

Wrapping my arms around her, I cup her breasts and give them a light squeeze. "You okay?"

"Yeah." She sighs, making it sound like she's not.

I give her a sympathetic frown.

"It was just a tough day. But you're here now." She runs her fingers across my forearms and rests her head back against my shoulder. "You're home, so everything's good again."

"Can I reinstate you to the role of mother again?"

She laughs. "Yeah, I guess I better not resign."

"Thanks." I kiss the tip of her nose and finally pull out of her. "I should get you into bed."

"Okay, but I'm not ready to sleep yet. I want to hear every detail of the game."

When she says shit like that, she actually means it. I'm going to have to give her a play-by-play of all my moves. At least the ones I can remember. She'll pepper me with questions and try to live the game through my recall of it.

As we put our pajamas on, she tells me she only caught snippets. Billy watched me for all of five minutes before getting distracted.

"I ran into the living room to try and see what I could, but the boys were..." She shakes her head. "It was just one of those days." She sniffs, her chin bunching for a moment. "Liam and Rachel popped in."

"Oh yeah?" I spin with surprise. "Rachel?"

"Yeah." Her expression buckles, and I can instantly tell there's more to this story. Caroline's smile is sad and wobbly.

Aw, shit. What the hell went down during that visit?

Caroline looks on the verge of tears again, and I know we'll have to talk about it. I open my mouth to say that, but she shakes her head.

"Let's talk hockey tonight." She sniffs. "I can tell you about my dumpster of a day tomorrow. I just want to fall asleep with good news in my head."

"You know we lost, right?"

She gives me a sad smile. "I know, and I'm sorry. But I saw you play for a couple minutes, and you were fire. I'm so proud of you."

My chest tingles with a warmth only she can ever give me.

We slip into bed and I hold her against me, the baby moving inside her as she rests her belly on my stomach. I feel those little kicks and my heart swells with anticipation. We still haven't decided what we're going to call our little angel yet, but we've got time to talk baby names. Right now, Caroline needs to talk hockey.

CHAPTER 13
BAXTER

"The goalie jerked left, sticking out his foot to stop the puck," I read to Kai. He's really getting into chapter books, and any story about hockey is king. Tammy's been working overtime to find books that fit his age and stage. He's actually a good little reader, but he prefers us to read to him, and I'm not complaining. It's one of my favorite times of the day.

Kai's snuggled up against my right side while Nova sits on my lap. She's sleepy, so she's in a cuddly mood. It's about the only time of day she sits still, and I always cherish these moments. Brushing my lips across her soft forehead, I keep reading to my kids while Tammy potters around in the kitchen. She's had a hectic week, but we're nearly at the finish line. Kai has one week left at school, and Tammy is taking a big chunk of time off this year. She's saved up vacation days so we can take a week off for our honeymoon and then spend another three full weeks with the kids after that. It's going to be the best summer. Asher's helped me find another handyman to plug the gaps while I'm away, and he's going to take over the admin side of my business for that month. I've got it all planned out.

We just have to make it through to the wedding and we'll be set.

I'm relieved that everything has gone so smoothly there. We're now just in that holding stage before all of the last-minute details need to get organized. The timing is going to be perfect, and I get a kick of excitement in my stomach every time I think about standing at the end of the aisle, watching Tammy walk toward me in whatever dress she's chosen. I still haven't seen it. Lani insisted that it was stored at her place, because the girls want it to be a surprise.

Fine. Whatever. I'm cool with that. For all I care, Tammy could walk down the aisle in a potato sack. She'd look good either way. I just want to stand there, watching her come toward me, *knowing* I'm about to make her officially mine.

We've got one month to go, and I'm tempted to start counting sleeps the way Kai always does.

Nova sniffs and rubs her nose against my shirt. I need to get her into bed soon. There's that perfect time window, and if you hit it just right, she'll sleep through until the morning, but if we leave it too late, she gets this second wind, but it's a grumpy, heinous one. More like a tornado that sweeps through the house, wreaking havoc.

"I need to get your sister to bed," I murmur to Kai.

"Not sweepy," she whines, rubbing her eyes.

I know better than to argue with her, so I simply kiss her head and go to stand.

"Not sweepy, Dada!" She fists my shirt. "Storwee! Storwee!"

"It's okay, Nova." Kai stands, rubbing his leg. "I'll read it to you in the morning, okay?" He goes on his tiptoes, giving her pudgy cheek a kiss before tickling her under the chin. She giggles, forgetting all her complaints. I give Kai a grateful wink.

Seriously. He's the best big brother in the world. Nova will do things for him that she'll never do for us.

I dance her into the kitchen, making her giggle some more as we waltz over the tiles.

"Bedtime?" Tammy grins, drying her hands and reaching up to give Nova a kiss. "Night, baby girl. I love you."

"Wuv you," Nova murmurs in her sweet little voice.

I kiss the top of her head and walk her down to her room. She's turning into a limp noodle, unable to fight her sleepy eyes. She keeps rubbing them and starts to grizzle against my shirt.

"Sleepy time," I whisper and start to hum the night-time song Tammy always sings to her. My voice isn't half as good as Mommy's, but Nova can feel the vibration in my chest as she snuggles into me.

We reach her bed, and she gives "staying up" one

more shot, but she can barely finish her sentence, the words fading away when her head hits the pillow.

"Love you, sweetheart," I whisper against her cheek, giving her a kiss and smiling down at her as she gives me a sleepy grin.

"Pancakes?" she mumbles.

"You want pancakes for breakfast?"

She nods, her blinks getting slower.

"Okay. You close your eyes and dream about pancakes, and we'll make some in the morning."

"'Kay, Dada."

"Love you," I whisper again, sure I will never get over how amazing the word *Dada* sounds coming out of her mouth.

I nearly cried the first time she said it. Yep, turns out I am the world's biggest softy when it comes to my daughter. Tammy can't help teasing me about it, but Nova's made me cry more than anyone. They're always happy, sentimental tears, but watching my own flesh and blood grow up is the most rewarding thing in my life. Kai feels like my own flesh and blood now, too, and I love that kid as much as I love his sister.

I'm a family man. Who would have guessed it? I had no idea how fulfilling it would be.

Now to make it all official.

I grin, padding back through to the living room. Kai's kept reading the book without me, and Tammy is on the phone, pacing and looking worried.

My protective instincts jump into high alert, and I move toward her with a questioning frown.

She shakes her head, closing her eyes with a sad sigh. "Yeah... no, I understand. Thanks for letting us know."

Hanging up, she passes my phone back to me, and I raise my eyebrows. "Who was that?" I glance at the screen.

"That was our reception venue."

I wince at the expression on her face. It matches her deflated tone perfectly.

"Uh-oh," I whisper.

"Yep." She nods, putting on a brave smile that turns into a trembling chin situation.

I pull her into my arms before she can start crying. "How bad is it?"

Her hands come around my waist, fisting my shirt at the back. "They had an electrical fire this morning."

"What?" I ping back to gape down at her.

"They're having to shut the place down while they renovate, and there's no way the repairs will be finished in time for our wedding." Her forehead crinkles, and a few tears splash out of her eyes. "It's happening again." She snivels. "The universe doesn't want us getting married, Bax. We should just—"

"Don't you dare say quit." I smile down at her. "I am making you my wife if it's the last thing I do." I kiss the tip of her nose. "I've loved you since I was a kid. I dreamed about marrying you in high school. This is happening, TT."

Her laugh is watery, her smile barely there. "I just don't know if I can do this again, you know? Deal with more problems around this wedding. Maybe we should just get married at a courthouse."

"No." I shake my head. "I know you want this wedding. *I* want this wedding, and we're going to make it happen. The church is still good to go; now we just have to find a new venue for the reception."

"And a caterer, and waitstaff, and—"

"Hey, slow down," I murmur softly. "One thing at a time."

She shakes her head, more tears spilling from her eyes. "My plate already feels so full leading up to this. The idea of having to spend hours sorting it all out..."

Kai gets up from the couch with a worried frown, nestling against her side. "It's okay, Mom. We'll find another venue. Let Dad and me figure it out."

"Sweet boy," she whispers, wrapping her arm around his shoulders and kissing his head.

The way he's been sprouting up over the past couple months, he's going to be taller than her in a year or two. He's grown so much since I first met him... and he's still the kindest kid I know.

Plus, he just called me Dad, and it doesn't matter how many times he says it, my heart fills to overflowing whenever he does. It's either Bax or Dad. I never know when the D-word will pop out, although it's happened a lot more since Nova was born... and I love it every time.

I'm feeling just a touch choked up as I wrap my arms

around both of them. "Kai's right. We're going to have this wedding. It's going to be amazing. We'll figure something out."

"How? The wedding is less than a month away. This is a small town. Everything will be booked." Tammy's voice pitches.

"We're going to make something work. There's bound to be somewhere that's available. Let Kai and me take this on. I don't want you to worry about a thing."

Tammy closes her eyes, resting her forehead against my chest.

I share a sad smile with Kai, but I can see the determination in his eyes. We're not going to let his mama down.

Which is why, once everyone's asleep, I creep back out of bed and decide to make a late-night phone call.

CHAPTER 14
ASHER

It's nearly eleven o'clock when my phone starts ringing. Lani and I are night owls, so it's no big deal, but my face bunches with concern when I notice it's Baxter. He always gets up so early and is usually lights out by like nine. I only know this because I've made the mistake of calling him at "ungodly" hours before. According to him, anything later than eight thirty is just plain rude.

I snicker, remembering that conversation as I swipe my thumb across my screen.

"Sup, man? You all good?"

"Not really." He sighs.

I glance at Lani, whose eyebrows rise in question. She moves from her reading chair and curls up beside me on the couch, leaning close so she can listen in. I wrap my arm around her knees and start trailing patterns across her smooth shins.

"There's been a fire at our reception venue." His voice is low and defeated.

"No way." I shake my head, and Lani starts making hand gestures that I take a little minute to interpret. "Hey, Bax. I'm just gonna put you on speakerphone, is that cool?"

"Yeah, I was hoping you and Lani can help me brainstorm ideas."

"Of course we can." She smiles. This is so her jam, and I can't help loving her with everything in me when I see her face light with animation as she slips into "problem-solving" mode. "What have you tried so far?"

"We only found out a few hours ago, and by the time Tammy stopped crying and I got Kai to bed, I haven't really had a chance to look at much. Tammy's so stressed about it that Kai and I agreed to take it on so she doesn't have to worry. But I'm not exactly sure where to start."

"One month is a tight timeframe, especially since it's summer, but we're bound to find something that can work." Lani starts listing off ideas, and Baxter rejects a few because he already knows they're taken.

"And I'm assuming you've already talked to Rachel about using Ponderosa," I pipe up.

"Yeah." He sighs. "It's already being used that weekend."

"We could ask the college if we could use the library or something." As soon as Lani suggests it, her nose wrinkles and she starts shaking her head. "But I'm not loving that idea. It's not right for you two."

Baxter lets out a breathy laugh. "It's not about the right feel, Lani. We just have to find something, even if it's not perfect."

"Oh, come on, Bax. Don't say that. Tammy deserves the best," Lani argues gently.

Baxter sighs. "I know. I just wish I knew how to give that to her."

We all go quiet for a minute, my brain scrambling to come up with something cool.

And then it hits me.

"What about the grove behind us? You know that cool area Fezzik loves so much."

Lani glances at me, her eyes lighting. "We could hang fairy lights between the tree branches."

"We could set up tables and chairs, then put a bunch of picnic blankets on the ground," I say, adding to her enthusiasm.

"What if it rains?" Baxter argues.

"What if it doesn't?" Lani counters, then tuts. "If it starts sprinkling, we'll all pull out our umbrellas. And if the bugs come out to play, we'll offer insect repellent as perfume. This will work, Bax. And it'll be beautiful." She grins. "We could do picnic baskets of food. It'll be so unique and different. I think people will love it. And I'm sure Rachel will be happy to help with catering. If it's picnic food, a lot of it can be made the day before." She goes through a bunch of practical ideas that Baxter can't refute, and by the time we wrap up the phone call, it's all set. She's buzzing, and even Baxter sounds like he might be smiling.

"Let's make this a surprise for her." He sounds kind of enthusiastic about the idea, while Lani winces.

"Do you think she'll be okay with that? I know if it were my wedding, I'd want to know what's going on."

"I think she's so over trying to make this thing happen, the thought of not having to think about it at all will make her happy. Let's aim for the surprise thing, and if I'm totally off the mark, we can pivot."

"Okay, man." I give him a thumbs-up, even though he can't see me. "We're looking forward to helping you pull this together."

"Thanks a lot, guys. I didn't know who else to call."

Lani gives me a mushy smile. "We're always here for you. You're family. We love you."

"Love you too," he mumbles before hanging up and no doubt blushing as red as a fire engine.

I skim my fingers over Lani's ear, then tuck her hair back over her shoulder. It's so long and luscious—a fruity-smelling ebony waterfall. I love burying my fingers in it.

She's gazing at me with this sweet smile, searching my face like she wants to ask me something serious or...

Oh shit. Is she gonna pop the question?

Like now?

No, she's not allowed to do that.

I've got a plan. I'm proposing! Screw her feministic

side. I want to be the guy who drops to one knee. I've got it all planned. I've booked a hot air balloon ride, and we're going to drift across the Nolan U campus. I'm going to tell her all my memories from our time at school together, and then once we're back on the ground, I'm going to jump out of the basket and present her with a ring.

It's all booked and paid for. She's not stealing this romantic moment from me.

"Well…" I force a yawn. "I'm actually kind of tired. It was a big day, meeting with clients and stuff. Think I might head to bed."

I jump off the couch like it's suddenly on fire, and Lani, without me to lean against anymore, topples onto the cushions.

Her head pops up and her eyes narrow, like she knows I'm up to something, but when she opens her mouth to speak, I start singing.

She probably thinks I'm possessed, but I don't know what else to do. Belting out the theme song from *Avengers*, I walk to the bathroom. "Dah-dah, dah, dah-na-na-dah…"

"You're so weird!" she calls after me.

"Thanks, boo." I raise my hand, not even turning to look back at her.

I hear a short huff and then what sounds like a cushion being thrown down to the ground.

It's hard not to grin as I step into the bathroom. I've gotten wind that she wants to ask me to marry her, but I bet you a million dollars her proposal is not as romantic as mine. She's got to let me have this one.

But knowing Lani, she won't.

Shit, she's probably going to refuse the fucking hot air balloon ride.

Dammit!

I should have just surprised her at work and popped the question weeks ago. But I want it to be epic. I want people to ask, "So, how did he propose?" and then for her to go on about how legendary and creative I am.

Is that really too much to ask?

Crouching down, I pull open the bottom drawer of the vanity, unearthing the ring box from the very back. Popping the lid, I gaze down at the ring I had specially designed. She's going to love it. Even if she's annoyed with me for proposing before she could, as soon as she sees this thing... she's gonna go weak at the knees.

"I'm winning this round, boo," I whisper with a grin, knowing deep down that as long as I get to marry this woman, I'm the ultimate winner, no matter how it plays out.

JUNE

CHAPTER 15
MIKAYLA

We're meeting one of my least favorite clients today. Ryan's convinced he's going to be the next big thing in baseball, but I find him to be an arrogant prick who thinks the sun shines out his ass, and every time I'm around him, I feel like I need to be wearing sunscreen—creep factor one billion.

He always sits across the table, watching me like I'm something to eat. It grosses me out.

Ryan signed him when I first started at the company, and I don't even know why I have to be at these stupid meetings, but he makes me come to every one of them.

I could be finishing off the stack of filing he gave me this morning and actually leave on time for once, but a gopher does what a gopher's told, and I ended up having to leave all that work in order to attend this meeting. Ryan probably still expects me to go back and finish it after the meeting, though. Oh joy.

He said these sessions are good training for me, so I should be grateful, but I don't know... I guess I'm not feeling it today. Or any day that I have to meet up with Axel Wayens.

It's been a shitty week, and I know I should be getting pumped for Tammy and Baxter's wedding, but I've got so much work on my plate. It's stressing me out and making me grumpy, and that's making Ethan grumpy, and... grrr. Life is just hard right now.

Straightening my cutlery the way Dad always does, I spin my wineglass around and tut when I realize I'm not wearing my rings again. Dammit! I must have left them on my nightstand. Ethan is going to be so pissed. I'll have to make sure I get home before him so I can slip them back on.

I've been making an extra effort to wear them since he's home more, now that the season has ended, but I was rushing out the door this morning and...

"Shit," I murmur, rubbing my ring finger and picturing my husband.

He's helping his dad with some overdue renovations and has been keeping busy being a handyman. He seems to be loving the time with his dad and comes home pretty happy. He left before I was awake this morning, wanting to fit in a workout before driving up to Denver.

The apartment felt cold and quiet without him... but that's nothing new either. During hockey season, I feel like he's never home. He is, but it just feels like he isn't, you know?

I wince and shake my head, wondering if he feels that way with my demanding job. I know it's pissing him off, but we've been making an effort to keep things upbeat and civil when we're around each other.

He still thinks I should quit, but he doesn't get it, and I don't want to keep arguing with him about it. He just has to accept that this job will take me places and—

"Hey, there." Axel—a.k.a. Mr. Baseball—saunters up to the table, giving me a cheesy smile.

I stand and greet him, shaking his hand. His palms are sweaty, and he always holds on for a beat longer than I like.

His eyes glint as he eyes me up and down, then shoots Ryan a grin. "You brought her."

"Just like you asked me to." Ryan smooths down his tie as we all take our seats.

"Excuse me?" I whisper to him.

Ryan lets out an awkward laugh, then gives me a pointed look and murmurs out the side of his mouth, "He likes you. Just go with it."

I don't even have time to gape at him before Axel's brushing his fingers over the top of my hand.

"So, how's it going?" He rests his elbow against the table, pushing his cutlery askew as he watches me.

"Good." I slide my hand away, tucking it under the table and trying for a smile. "How are things with you, Mr. Wayens?"

He tips his head back with a laugh. "Please. It's Axel.

Come on, girl. Don't treat me like that. We're friends, you and me. You're my agent."

"Actually, Ryan's your agent, and I'm his assistant."

"Which makes you my agent." Axel bulges his eyes at me like I'm stupid.

I can't believe I'm being made to feel like a fool by this dipshit.

Shifting in my seat, I pull out the folder Ryan made me bring and flip it open. "So, let's get down to business."

"What's the rush?" He leans back in his seat, picking up his menu and taking forever to peruse it.

I shoot Ryan a side-eye, frowning at him as soon as Axel's phone rings and he gets distracted.

He leans across to me. "I knew you'd get all pissy if I told you at the office, but I need you here. I really want Axel to sign with this new sporting goods company, and since he likes you so much, he'll probably do it if you ask him to. I sent him the pitch, and he said he'd get back to me, but he's taking forever to make a decision. The offer's only on the table for a short time before they look elsewhere."

I frown at him. "What do you mean, he likes me?"

"Ever since he saw you at the office that day, he's been gaga over you. He asks about you all the time."

What the fuck?

"So that's why you make me come to all of these stupid, uncomfortable meetings?" I glare at him, darting my eyes to make sure Axel's still distracted.

"Well, duh. You've got to be useful for something."

And now a second man is looking at me like I'm stupid today.

I growl in my throat and go to lean away, but he snatches my shirt sleeve and pulls me back.

"Hey, this is a great opportunity for you. Think of these meetings as tutorials. You'll be doing this on your own one day, and you need to know how to sway a client in the direction you want him to go."

I wrinkle my nose but am slightly appeased by the fact that he thinks I will eventually get somewhere one day. The thought of being an agent and having my own clients who I can support gives me a little thrill.

"Now, you sell him on this deal, you hear me? We need this. Remind him about the presentation. Tell him we need an answer by the end of this lunch." I clench my jaw, my nostrils flaring as Ryan adds in another punch to the gut. "Be flirty. Make him think he's the best thing since Babe Ruth."

Okay, thrill killed, good feelings gone. I want to strangle Ryan right about now.

Be flirty?

I'm a married woman!

I want to hold up my rings and show him, but of course I'm not wearing them. Fuck!

It's tempting to call Ethan and have him crash this meeting, but that would make me look so unprofessional, and I have to prove to him that I can handle this job.

Axel finishes his phone call, and all I can feel is Ryan's

laser beam gaze as I force another smile at the baseball player and try to be charming.

"You're a popular man."

He holds up his phone with a grin. "The ladies love me."

"I'm sure they do." Shit, keeping this smile in place is hurting my chin... and cheeks... and lips!

I brush my teeth over my bottom lip and try to get straight to the point.

"So, this deal that we pitched to you last month is really promising. You remember the presentation, right? I mean, these guys are going to make you look good." I draw out the last word, half singing it, and add in a laugh that sounds cringingly plastic. Hoping he doesn't notice how fake I'm sounding, I rush forward with my pitch. "They're willing to throw a lot of money at you too. And all they're asking in return is a photo shoot and one appearance at their new store opening."

He wrinkles his nose, slumping back in his chair. "Yeah, I don't know. They seem kind of small-time, you know?"

That's because you're *kind of small-time, dumbass!*

The guy is hoping to make the majors next season, but that all depends on how he plays this summer. If he can have a killer minor league season—which he's on track for—then the majors are a given. The MLB is already showing interest, and he would have been plucked right out of college if it hadn't been for that DUI incident his senior year. He's had to pay his dues and got picked up by a minor league team instead, much to his angst. He should have been grateful, the little shit, but he bitched and moaned until Ryan persuaded him to have a killer season that will make the MLB so jealous, they'll regret not drafting him immediately.

I tilt my head and catch his eye, my smile bright and no doubt nauseously cheesy. "There's nothing wrong with getting a little sponsorship to help you through the rest of this year. The fact that companies are interested in you reflects well, you know? The league will notice the fact that you're already getting sponsorship deals."

He purses his lips. "I don't really like their clothing."

I shoot a glance at Ryan, but he nudges me under the table. His little foot tap is ordering me to sell this... to prove myself.

"Axel, come on." Shit, I sound like a used cars salesman. "We all know you'll look good in anything. Your pretty face is gonna be plastered all over the shop and their socials. Plus, you're bound to get a bunch of fans showing up to the opening of their new store. You could take some selfies, sign some baseballs... it'll be cool. Great PR."

He tips his head, his shoulder hitching. "It's no Nike or Adidas."

You're not Babe Ruth, you little fuckwit!

Leaning over the table, he reaches for my hand, and my skin crawls as I let him take it, let him brush his thumb over my skin and smile at me like I'm his favorite treat. "You really think I should do it?"

"Yeah. I think it'd be good for you. Your career."

"Will you come to the opening with me?"

I swallow, resisting the urge to rip my hand out from under his. "As your agent's assistant, I will make every effort to be there."

"She'll be there." Ryan grins, resting his elbows on the table and looking hopeful.

Shooting him a glare, he ignores my silent fury and prattles on about how great Axel is and how beneficial a partnership will be with this company.

I finally get my hand back, using the excuse to go to the bathroom. I don't need to pee, but I wash my hands with soap and rest against the vanity, gazing at my reflection with a hopeless sigh.

My phone starts ringing and I fish it out of my pocket, my insides jumping with comfort when I spot Ethan's number.

"Hey, Tall Man."

"Lil' mouse." He's smiling. I can hear it in his voice. "How's it going?"

"Yeah, all right," I mutter.

"You at the office?"

"No," I grumble. "I'm at this stupid lunch with one of Ryan's clients."

"I thought you liked meeting clients. Isn't that the best part of the job?"

"Usually, but not all clients are created equal."

"Oh." I bet he's nodding with understanding right now. An ache for him blooms inside me. I want to be there with him at his dad's house, getting covered in sawdust and paint and— "So, what's wrong with this client? Can you say, or are they right there?"

"I'm in the bathroom." I spin around, resting my butt against the edge of the vanity. "He's a bit arrogant, and... I don't know." I shrug. "It's not the fun, cocky arrogant that you are."

He snickers.

"This guy thinks he's God's gift to all women."

"Well, at least he knows you're taken."

I glance down at my hand, guilt riding through me. "Yeah." I rub my thumb over my ring finger and wince, forgetting myself as I mumble, "Not sure it'd make a difference, though."

"What?" Ethan's voice sharpens, and I instantly register what I just said. "Is that asshole making moves on you?"

Shit! I snap my eyes closed. "Not really. It's nothing I can't handle."

"Which means he is, and you're hiding in the bathroom to get away from him!" he growls. "Where are you?"

"Nope." I shake my head. "Ethan, you can't come in and disrupt this meeting."

"I can if that guy is putting hands on you and making you feel uncomfortable! You shouldn't be tolerating that shit, Mikayla!"

"I'm not!" I argue back and cringe at what a fucking lie that is. "I just have to get him to sign this deal, and then I can leave. I can handle it."

"He better not fucking touch you."

I sigh. "Stop acting like such a caveman."

"I thought you liked my caveman side."

A soft snort pops out my nose. "I don't mind a little growling and you throwing me over your shoulder, but I have a big issue with you storming into a restaurant and disrupting a work meeting."

He huffs, and I can picture him running a hand through his hair. "I hate that you're having to put up with this shit, Mick."

"Look, this is what it takes, okay? I have to schmooze and cajole and—"

"I wish you would quit."

Anger fires through me, and I ping straight. "Would you stop asking me to do that!"

"Well, I'm sorry, but any job where you have to play nice with some asshole just so he'll sign a fucking piece of paper is dumb. You shouldn't have to flirt with some moron to get what you want. You're married to me, and I know how much you hate this shit. Just quit already."

"And do what?" I snap back. "Just give up on my dream?"

"It's not your dream," he mumbles.

"I told you when we first met that I wanted to be a sports agent. If I quit, what the hell am I? Some heinous hockey wife whose biggest concern is getting her nails done in time for the game?" Okay, great, now I'm shouting, and my voice sounds so scathing that even my skin's starting to crawl.

Ethan sighs, and I can sense him reining it in. His father must have just walked into the room or something, because his tone lowers to a soft, husky whisper. "You say this is your big dream, but it's not. You didn't want this. You wanted to be a sports agent who represents athletes who deserve a shot, not arrogant fuckwits who think they're God's gift. Why are you compromising?"

"Because reality kicked in, and this was the only job I could get, okay?" I spin and catch my reflection, my eyebrows dipping into a sharp V. "Everywhere I wanted to go said I needed experience, so that's what I'm getting. Life isn't always handed to us on a silver platter. I know you can't relate to that, because everything you touch turns to gold, but it's not like that for the rest of us."

He lets out a scoff that makes it abundantly clear I've insulted him. Shit. I need to end this call before I say something else I'll regret.

"Look, I've got to go and finish this deal. Everything going okay with your dad?"

He's silent for a painful beat and I brace myself for another attack, but in the end, he sighs and mutters, "Things are tracking great here. I'll be back home by six. You gonna be there for dinner?"

"That's the plan," I murmur, wrapping my arm around my waist and trying not to notice how my lips are trembling as I say goodbye to my husband and brace myself to meet with Mr. Baseball again.

Ugh.

It takes me another hour of convincing before he finally caves—thank fuck!

As soon as I step back into the office, Sean is on me to finish the work I hadn't completed because he needs it ASAP.

I work my ass off, forgetting time until Ryan flicks off his office light and tells me to have a good one.

Glancing at my clock as he walks out the door, I feel my entire body deflate.

I'm two hours late... and Ethan never called to find out where I am.

He probably tracked me on my phone, saw I was still at the office, and is sitting at home, fuming because once again I'm letting him down.

I rush to finish up the contract, slamming it onto my boss's desk before running for my car. I'm the last person here, so I have to lock up and alarm everything, which makes me even later, and by the time I burst through our apartment door, I'm a frazzled mess.

"I'm here, I'm here, I'm here!"

I'm met with stone-cold silence.

"Ethan?"

The bag slips off my shoulder with a thump, and I check each room before finding the table all set. Dinner for two is laid out beautifully—there's even a bunch of red roses on the table—but the burritos are cold, and sitting next to the vase of fresh flowers is a note.

. . .

I waited for two hours and couldn't do it anymore.

Hope you got that contract signed.

I've headed up to Nolan to hang with the guys for a bit. They're having a bachelor party for Baxter, and I don't want to miss it.

It'll give you a chance to focus solely on work until the rehearsal dinner.

Love you xx

Plunking into my chair, I gaze at the note and don't even know what to think... or feel.

Why didn't he call me?

Because he's pissed and hurt and—

I snap my eyes shut, crumpling the note in my hand and throwing it onto the floor. No one said married life would be easy, but does it have to be this fucking hard?

CHAPTER 16
LANI

Okay, today's the day.

No matter what, I'm proposing.

I can sense Asher has something big brewing, and he's trying to outsmart me. Things have been unusually tense between us as we both try to avoid each other so we can't spoil any surprises we've planned, but I decided last night as we celebrated Tammy's bachelorette party, and swooned over her upcoming nuptials, that I couldn't delay this any longer. The best way to surprise my man is to forget about all the elaborate ideas I've been toying with and just freaking ask him!

I don't want to take away from Tammy and Baxter's big day next weekend, and I'm guessing Asher is thinking the same. He probably has some grand plan which he'll show me, maybe even the day after the wedding, but I don't need anything fancy.

Why should guys always get to propose anyway?

I'm doing it today and have spent the last two hours setting up the top floor of the villa. I've lit enough candles in our bedroom and the living room to put the fire station on high alert and have classical music wafting out of the speakers. I've spent all week compiling the perfect playlist—selecting all of the most romantic classical music I could find.

I bought all of Asher's favorite treats—the coffee table is piled high—plus I wrote a quiz. Just ten quick questions, the last one being... Will you marry me?

Sweet, simple, and romantic.

Tick, tick, tick.

I'm grinning as I pad down the hallway, heading into the bathroom so I can double-check my makeup and put on Asher's favorite dress. Then I'll—

"Lani?" Asher's surprised voice reaches me from the living room.

Shit, he's back early. I didn't even hear him coming up the stairs!

I run out to find him, my bathrobe flying open because I forgot to tie it back up...

And there he is in a tuxedo, holding a large bunch of roses and gaping at me.

His eyes heat with desire as they travel down my body. Yes, I'm in my lacy black lingerie. And is he about to...?

"Don't you dare get down on one knee," I warn him, pointing my finger with the sternest look I can muster.

He narrows his eyes at me, glancing around the living room, then arching his brow.

"Leilani Iona, will you—"

"Marry me?" I pop out the question before he can.

His face bunches into a scowl and he goes to drop to one knee, but I fall to the floor—yes, still in my underwear—and quickly rush out, "Asher Bensen, will you—"

"Marry me?" he interrupts, and I huff, jumping back to my feet and resting my hands on my hips.

"Will you marry me?" we both blurt in unison, then end up growling.

The bouquet of roses hits Asher's leg, some of the petals falling to the floor. "Dammit, woman. Can't you just let me propose? I got you a ring!"

"Yeah, well, me too!" I flick my arm at him. "Why should you get to be the only one to gift the person you love a beautiful piece of jewelry!"

He goes still, blinking at me and suddenly fighting a grin. "You got me a ring?"

"Yes," I mumble, pulling my bathrobe around myself and tying it securely.

"Can I see it?" He lays the roses down on the table, eyeing the food before grinning at me. "Did you bake it into the chocolate cake?"

"Ewww, no." I scrunch up my nose, then sigh, my own lips starting to quirk up at the edges. "I'll let you see it if you let me propose."

He rolls his eyes, sucking in a breath and holding it like he's counting to ten.

I arch my eyebrow at him.

"Okay, fine. But then I get to propose after you."

"Fine." I roll my eyes, but my giggle is soft and uncontrolled as I walk to the coffee table and dig the ring box out of my prize bag. "I wrote a quiz, and I was going to give you a little prize after each correct answer."

"Really?" His voice perks up. "I love that idea. Hit me, boo."

I stare at him for a second, loving his enthusiasm as he takes a seat on the couch and flicks his fingers at me.

"Okay, fine." I nod and pull out my question cards. "Which constellations did we talk about the first night we made love?"

Asher tips his head back, his eyes snapping shut. "That would be Orion and Scorpius."

"Very good." I grin, pulling a black G-string out of the bag and throwing it at him.

He holds it up with a smirk. "This is my prize?"

"You can rip it off me later." I wink, and he starts laughing.

"Well, bring on question two, then!"

I giggle. "What's my favorite dessert?"

"Crème brûlée."

"What's my real favorite dessert?"

He grins. "Oreo ice cream with way too much chocolate sauce."

"Correct and correct." I throw him a bottle of chocolate sauce, and he wiggles his eyebrows at me.

I continue asking him questions that prove he knows me better than anybody else and makes me want to marry him more now than I ever have before.

Flipping to the next card, I pull in a breath, smile down at the question, and then look him in the eye.

"Question ten," I whisper.

His gaze turns soft and mushy.

"Will you make me the happiest woman on this earth and marry me?"

"Yes." His voice is a sexy, husky whisper, and I feel my insides tremble as a watery laugh punches out of me.

"Correct answer." I reach into the prize bag and pull out the small box. Holding it out for him, I can't take my eyes off his face as he pops it open.

His lips part, this soft, awe-filled sound escaping him as he pulls out the tungsten ring inlayed with a line of small rubies.

"Red rubies," he murmurs, his voice kind of choked up.

"For Gryffindor," we whisper at the same time.

His gaze jumps up to meet mine, and I've never been more sure of anything in my entire life—I'm staring at my soulmate. And he just said yes!

I'm going to marry my soulmate!

He sniffs, blinking as he lets me slip the ring on.

"It looks so good on you." I brush my fingers over his, and he captures my hand, threading our fingers together and smiling at me.

"I love you so much."

I want to say the same, but my throat has gone all thick. He's about to propose!

"When I first met you..." He laughs and shakes his

head. "I thought you were such a piece of work. No one has ever put me in my place the way you have. I thought I couldn't stand you, but it took all of one drive and a quiz night to be totally enamored with you. And every day, I find another reason to love you. Every month that passes, I become even more sure that I can't live without you."

My heart trills, tears clogging my throat at the look of pure adoration on his face.

"You're the best thing that's ever happened to me."

"You too," I squeak.

He grins. "Wanna be my wife forever and ever?"

"Yes," I blubber, lurching forward and planting my lips on his. He lets go of my hands, holding my face and swiping his tongue into my mouth. It's a deep, passionate kiss filled with hope and promise.

He eases away, brushing his nose against mine before pulling a box from his jacket pocket.

"Your ring, milady." He pops it open for me, and my heart skips through my chest, a soft gasp popping out of my mouth, followed by a wispy laugh.

"Ravenclaw," I whisper, staring at the stunning sapphire ring.

"You know it, boo." He laughs, pulling the ring out to slip it onto my finger. "It's so funny that we thought of the same thing."

"I know." My stomach trembles from laughter or tears —I can't tell. My emotions are running so high that I feel lightheaded. "We're so meant to be."

He grins, gazing at the ring on my finger and nodding. "Yeah, we are."

I stare at the ring, studying it from every angle with an awe-filled smile. "Can you believe we're finally engaged?"

"We have taken way too long to make this happen. Seriously, why were we so stubborn over this thing?"

I groan and tip my head back. "Because the idea of planning a wedding is so overwhelming. I just couldn't do it. As soon as people find out, the pressure will instantly come on. You know what it's like. Everyone who loves us means well, but..." I wince.

"I feel ya." He nods. "My mother will be a nightmare."

My wince deepens as I squeak, "She will."

He laughs and brushes his thumb across my cheek. "Well, let's just keep things quiet for a bit. We don't want to take away from Tammy and Baxter's big day anyway. Why don't we go to the rehearsal dinner on Friday night and not wear the rings? Then a few days after the wedding is over and they've had their big moment, we can slip them on again. We don't have to announce anything. If someone is smart enough to notice the rings, we can tell them then."

"Agreed." I rub my thumb over his band, then go to take my stunning ring off.

"Wait, wait, wait." He stops me. "Once I've made love to my fiancée, then you can take it off."

My lips rise into what I hope is a playful, sexy smirk. "You want to make love to me with our rings on?"

His hooded eyes make me feel like my skin's on fire. "Boo, that's the only thing I want you wearing." His deft fingers quickly untie my robe, and he flicks it open, exposing my lacy lingerie. "Damn, woman," he whines, his eyes drinking me in. "What you do to me."

With a soft growl, he launches out of his seat, cinching me around the waist and lifting me off the couch. I can't help a laughing squeal as he walks me to the wooden table, which is sometimes a desk and sometimes a dining table. He places me onto the polished surface. The wood hits my naked butt cheeks and I yelp at the contact but am soon distracted by a luscious tongue gliding into my mouth. His strong hands wrap about the back of my neck, his fingers fisting my hair as he kisses me soundly, overriding all my senses.

I start yanking at his jacket, shoving it off his shoulders and loving the sound of each item hitting the floor. The living room is soon littered with fabric, my bra dangling off the bookshelf as Asher sucks my eager nipple into his mouth. I moan, fisting his hair and thrusting my chest toward him. He plays with my sensitive body, drawing patterns on my skin and using his teeth to pull the lace off me. I lie back, the cold desk barely registering as I lift my hips. My G-string ends up bunched around my ankle and I flick it off, giggling to myself as it arcs through the air and gets caught on the lampshade.

Asher gazes down at me, his hungry eyes making my skin tingle. Parting my legs, he devours my pussy without even touching me. His searing stare makes me feel like the sexiest woman on the planet.

His lips rise into that delectable smirk of his, and I grin at him as he lightly kisses my knee, then starts working his way down to my sensitive haven. His tongue destroys me, knocking out the power to most of my brain. All that remains is the heady ecstasy of his tongue lapping my pussy before he gently sucks my clit between his lips. I groan, fisting his hair and pressing my toes into the desk. He scoops his hands under my butt, giving it a squeeze and pulling my folds apart. His tongue pancakes over me, long licks from the base to my clit until my breaths are a frenzied mess. Shock waves pulse though my body as he grips my ass even tighter, then sucks my clit again.

I pinch my nipples, breaths punching out of me as I arch my back and revel in his practiced touch. He knows all my hot spots, and he's hitting each one with his expert tongue. I can't control my voice as an orgasm builds, burning through me as cries of pleasure rise in my throat.

"That's it, boo," he murmurs around my clit before pressing his thumb against it. "Come for me."

I let out another cry, my inner walls spasming as my body starts to quiver. I revel in this moment, my body jerking uncontrollably as I'm taken out from all sides. My chest is heaving, my heart thundering when I hit my high with gusto.

"You're so fucking sexy, fiancée." Asher grins down at me.

"I love you," I manage to whisper. "I'm so fucking glad you're gonna be my husband."

He grabs my hips, sliding me to the edge of the table. I sit up, pulling his face toward me and thrusting my tongue into his mouth. We moan in unison, his hands gliding around my back as I deepen the kiss even more. It's like we want to crawl inside each other. I could find a happy home in his chest.

"I've got to have you, baby," he murmurs between kisses. "Let me take you right here."

I pull away from him, spreading my legs and giving him easy access to my body. His cock is rigid, standing at attention, and I watch it with a grin, scraping my teeth across my bottom lip as he parts my folds and lines himself up.

His head hits my wet core, and I grip his shoulders, silently urging him deeper.

He reads my mind and gives me a deep, strong thrust that has me moaning all over again.

I love this man. I love him inside me.

My eyes pop open and I spot my ring, glistening against his skin as he thrusts once more.

I love his ring on my finger.

I love my ring on his.

Lying back, I lift my legs, and he places them against his shoulders. His soft fingers wrap around my ankles as he plunges again.

His groan overrides the classical music sweeping over us, and I tune in to it, becoming acutely aware of every sound our bodies make together—the rhythmic beat of our coupling, the whimper that stirs in his throat, that guttural groan that rips out of mine when he pushes my legs forward and changes the angle.

He slows his pace for a moment, shortening his thrusts so he can work my G-spot and send my body into another frenzy.

My moans escalate, my chest heaving as I bite my bottom lip and tip my head back.

Spreading my arms wide, I grip the edge of the table when he plunges deep again, then goes a little harder, a little faster, until I'm consumed by him.

His fingers dig into my ass and he practically pulls me off the table, hips pumping like a piston as he speeds toward his orgasm.

"Oh fuck. Fuck." He breathes the words, his body convulsing before he lets out a strangled cry and jerks inside me, then plunges to his hilt. Snatching my ankles, he squeezes them and thrusts a few more times.

I can feel him going off, his seed spurting into me as I cling to the table and ride out this wild storm of pleasure.

He's always been able to make me breathless. To send me over the edge. And once again, he's won first prize.

Or maybe I have.

Because surely marrying this man makes me the ultimate winner in all things.

CHAPTER 17
LIAM

My shift has less than an hour to go. The rain has been falling steadily all day, and I'm definitely ready to finish up and go see my woman. She'll be at the wedding rehearsal now. I wanted to go with her, but in order to get tomorrow off, I had to work today. I'll catch her at the rehearsal dinner tonight, but I'm looking forward to that. It's been such a long time coming, and they've had so many things get in their way, but tomorrow... it's happening. I've never seen Baxter more determined about anything.

Rachel's been working her ass off preparing food and helping Lani and Asher set up the grove with fairy lights and picnic tables. It's been good for her. It's helped to distract her from the torture of waiting to hear from the adoption agency again.

I was so gutted when the last one fell through. I couldn't really show it, because Rachel was struggling so much and needed me to be strong, but it was like a punch to the heart. I thought I was finally going to be a dad, but yet again, it wasn't happening.

Sometimes I worry that the universe doesn't want me to be a father. It's not like I had a very good one—no decent example to follow—and I'm still a little terrified that I might turn out like him, which is why I don't drink alcohol.

But I don't want that hurting Rachel. She would be the best mother—so loving, sweet, and kind. She deserves to have a baby, and I hate that our bodies won't let us do that. When the IVF didn't work, it was gut-wrenching, after the amount of money we poured into it. I still owe Mikayla's dad, but he keeps telling me there's no rush.

"It's an interest-free loan to pay back in your own time. Please don't stress yourself out about it."

We're currently paying him back a thousand dollars a month, and it's going to take forever at this rate. Thank God that adoption grant came through. Even with that, we've all but emptied our savings account to make this happen. So... it needs to fucking happen.

Holding my sigh in check, I glance at my partner, sitting in the driver's seat and texting who knows. We're parked across the road from the college, watching summer students dash through the rain.

I'm working with Dan today, and he's always after low-key shifts, so we'll often park in places like this and while away the hours waiting for a call. Rain can sometimes bring out the worst in people, but all we've had to deal with today is a shoplifter at the drugstore and a neighborly dispute over a barking dog.

I glance at my watch. Forty-three minutes to go. I'm nearly home clear.

"Unit Five, we have a 10-50 on Indigo and Twenty-Seventh. Multiple injuries. Possible fatality. Ambulance has been dispatched."

Road accident. I wince, grabbing for the radio as Dan pulls away from the curb. "Copy that, dispatch. En route to scene."

I flick on the sirens and the rain picks up, the wipers slashing across the windshield as we speed through town. Traffic makes way and we arrive four minutes later, my insides dropping as I spot the mangled car and steam rising from the crumpled hood. A dented delivery truck is sitting at an odd angle, obviously having plowed into the vehicle and sent it spinning into a lamppost. I have no idea who's at fault, but the poor car didn't stand a chance against that truck.

"Dispatch, Unit Five arrived on scene. What's the ETA on that ambulance?"

"Two minutes out."

"Copy that."

I slip out of the squad car, pulling my hat down as I approach the two vehicles and the five civilians working hard to wrench doors open and gain access to the injured passengers. There's a frantic energy buzzing between them as they shout suggestions at one another. I glance at the truck, noticing the crumpled door askew and then spotting a few people crouching down beside the shaken driver. He's sitting on the curb, someone holding a T-shirt to his head, failing to mop up the stream of blood pouring from the gash along his hairline. His eyes are dazed and glassy, his skin pale.

"Keep pressure on it," I call to the helpful woman. "The paramedics will be here in just a minute."

I then turn my attention back to the car.

"Okay, what have we got here?" I ask the guy closest to me, my stomach plummeting when I notice the limp limbs at unnatural angles and the blood smeared across the cracked glass.

"I didn't even see it happen." The man's voice trembles as he moves back from the door he's failing to open. "I just heard the almighty smash and came running."

"You three, step back, please. We don't want any more injuries. Watch that glass!" Dan starts ordering the crowd around while I take a closer look into the written-off car.

From my brief glance, I can't imagine there being much hope for the driver or the passenger, but I still pull on a pair of disposable gloves and pick my way around to the smashed window on the other side of the mangled wreck. One of the guys is arguing with Dan, insisting that he keep helping us.

As I reach in to examine the driver, I hear a soft wail, and my insides jolt.

"There are kids in there!" the man bellows at Dan.

Poking my head into the vehicle, I see the two car seats, and my stomach plummets.

Holy shit.

Racing to the back door, I try to wrench it open. My movements are frantic, the mangled metal making it impossible to budge the door.

"Dan, get over here!" I shout, willing my muscles to be stronger as I strain against this stubborn door.

He's already on his way, the determined civilian following in his wake. My partner blinks against the rain and peers through the back window.

"Shit," he mutters, coming to help me as the kids inside obviously pick up on our panic and start wailing in earnest.

The boy, who looks to be about three, is letting out these gasping sobs while his baby sister is kicking her legs and screaming. His cries are triggering hers, and I can feel their terror.

"That thing isn't moving," Dan puffs, resting his hand on his hip. "But it's too dangerous to break the glass, and we can't move those bodies either. Sir, would you please step back."

"We need to get those kids out of there." The man looks distraught.

"I know. Sir, we're gonna get them out. Do you know these kids?"

"No." He shakes his head. "But I have a young son, and I..." He points to the car.

"Okay." Dan gently ushers him away from the car.

I stare at the crumpled mess and curse under my breath, pulling the radio off my belt and contacting the station.

"Dispatch, this is Unit Five. We've got children trapped in this vehicle. Need urgent assistance."

"Fire is on the way. They've been delayed by another call out but should be there in five minutes."

I slip my radio back onto my belt, then bend down to try and get the boy's attention. "Hey, buddy!" I tap on the glass, swiping rain off my face. "Can you hear me?"

He stops screaming for a second, poking his head around the edge of his car seat so he can get a better look at me.

"Hi." I wave my hand, smiling and wondering how distorted I must look through the splintered glass. "I know you're scared," I call to him. "But we're going to get you out of there, okay? I'm a police officer, and I'm here to help you."

His big brown eyes gape at me for a long beat, and then he starts wailing again. His poor little sister hasn't stopped, and I feel helpless as I stand here waiting for support.

The ambulance arrives, the paramedics running to do their jobs, and thank God the fire crew turns up only moments later.

Dan and I work crowd control, two other units arriving to support us while I anxiously wait for those kids to be freed from the wreckage.

Dan's questioning witnesses, and I should be, too, but

I've just heard the deafening sound of screeching metal. I run back to the car, ready to grab those kids as soon as they come out.

The firefighter pulls the baby seat out, and I rest it in the crook of my elbow, then scoop the little boy into my arms as soon as he's clear of the vehicle. Walking them through the driving rain to the squad car, I open the back door and get them inside.

The poor little girl has screamed herself back to sleep and is now whimpering, her little chest heaving as her brother climbs over my lap and stares down at her.

"Is this your little sister?"

Tears splash out of his eyes as he nods.

"She's safe now," I assure him.

The boy glances at me.

"What's her name?"

He stares at me for a long, slow beat before finally whispering, "Lucia."

"That's a pretty name." I smile, running my hand down his back. "And what's your name?"

"Carlos." He has a mild accent, so I decide to greet him in Spanish.

"Hola, Carlos."

His head snaps around to face me, his eyes wide. I give him a soft smile and start speaking to him in Spanish.

I find out that he's three.

And that his favorite color is blue.

It takes me about twenty minutes to get that much. He

keeps looking out the window and staring at the crumpled car. I don't want him to see his parents' mangled bodies, so I distract him with my flashlight, keeping his face turned away as they're pulled from the wreckage and covered with white sheets.

My stomach knots into a hard ball when Carlos starts crying again. A whimper bubbles out of his throat, and then the tears fall in earnest all over again. He flops against my chest, and I cradle his head, singing a Spanish lullaby and trying to calm him.

The rain eases to a gentle whisper, running down the glass as I stare at the heartbreaking scene and wait for the paramedics to come check on the children. Child services will no doubt meet us at the hospital and get these kids someplace safe for the night.

I hope they have grandparents or aunts and uncles nearby who can take them in.

These two precious kids have just lost their parents in one fell swoop.

How can life be so monumentally unfair?

CHAPTER 18
ETHAN

Mikayla arrives at the rehearsal dinner looking so stunning my chest hurts. Her hair's up in a stylized pony-tail thing, and she's got these long, dangly earrings swishing against her shoulders. And then there's the dress—holy fuck, the dress! It's midnight blue, hugging her curves in all the right ways and only just covering her ass. I'm mesmerized by her hips, watching them sway as she walks toward me. Then I glance up at her face and the air gets stolen right out of my lungs.

Damn, I've missed her. It's been a shitty couple days in Nolan without her, and although we've texted a few times, we haven't spoken, and the stone in my stomach is getting heavier by the day.

She gives me a brief, closed-mouth smile, adjusting her dress as she walks toward me. She's in heels, so I don't have to bend down so far to kiss her. My hand trails along her curves, lightly squeezing her ass as we pull back from the kiss.

"Hey." Her eyes dart up to mine, then quickly away.

Shit, I shouldn't have just left her the way I did—the note on the table was a bit of a dick move—but I was pissed. And it's not like she's apologized for saying she'd be home and then not communicating with me at all. Does she expect me to just sit around the house waiting for her all the time?

Regret and anger vie for top position in my chest, and I don't know which to settle on.

Her small fingers thread between mine, and she pulls me into the restaurant before I can tell her how pretty she looks.

Fuck. What is happening to us?

We're physically connected, yet I've never felt so far from her.

Our relationship has always been this fun, upbeat thing... and I hate the place we're in right now. There's no laughter and teasing. Fuck, we're barely smiling at each other. And it's all because of her fucking job. It's stealing my wife away, and it kills me that I don't know how to stop it.

"Yay, you made it." Tammy laughs, pulling Mikayla in for a hug. "You look so freaking gorgeous!"

Mikayla smiles at her, brushing her hand through the air with a "this old thing?" expression on her face.

Tammy shakes her head. "Don't go selling yourself short. You're hot, girl. Own it."

Dipping her hip with a little laugh, she takes the compliment, but I can tell she's tense. I miss my girl. How the fuck do I get her back?

"Mick." Rachel glides over, her long dress billowing out around her legs as she walks our way. She pulls her friend into a tight hug, and they murmur shit I can't hear.

I turn, raising my chin at Casey, who beckons me over to his table.

The guys have been a great support the last couple days. I opened up a little before Baxter's bachelor party, which kind of put a downer on things, but I solved that problem by getting rip-roaring drunk and waking up in the Ponderosa pool house with a monster headache and pretty blurry memories of the night before.

Liam was kind enough to feed me Advil and water for the morning. Rachel made me this weird-ass smoothie that was green but tasted okay. I was feeling semi-coherent by lunchtime and decided to hang with Asher and Lani for a bit, but then I spent the whole time watching the irritating smiles they kept giving each other. They have some secret joke or something between them, and it's really starting to grate on my nerves. It's like they're more loved up than the last time I saw them, and it's pissing me off because I've never felt so distant from Mikayla, and she's my *wife*. Asher and Lani aren't even fucking engaged, let alone married!

Fuck!

Slumping back in my chair, I try to hide the torrent ripping through me. I can play pretend, right? No one needs to know that Mick and I are struggling. It's just a phase, isn't it? Once she finally gets her head on straight and quits this damn job, we'll find our mojo again.

What if she never quits?

My insides pinch into a painful knot, and it's an effort to raise my lips into a smile when she finally takes a seat next to me. She took her sweet time, talking to Rachel for ages until Liam arrived.

I snatch my chance to connect with her and softly whisper against her ear, "Rachel all good? I noticed some tension between her and Caroline."

"Baby stuff," she mouths, and I know better than to ask for details right now. Poor Liam and Rachel have been trying for years, while Casey and Caroline are popping out babies left and right.

Liam did mention that they're looking into adoption, but I haven't heard the latest. He texted before to say he was running late, and now that he's here, I want to ask him more. "Work emergency" was all Rachel could tell me when I arrived at the restaurant.

She didn't seem too flustered by it. I guess she's used to him working overtime. So why the hell do I get so bothered by Mick's overtime?

Because she doesn't get paid for it.

Because Liam's a cop and doesn't have control over when people decide to be idiots. It's not like he can walk away from an emergency. Mick doesn't have emergencies at her job!

Waiters start bringing out food, and I pick at my meal. I want to devour this shit because it's delicious, but my stomach is too tense. Mikayla seems to be the same and even offers me a roast potato off her plate. She's barely touched a quarter of the food, but I shake my head. She frowns at my refusal. When am I not stealing food off her plate?

When my insides feel like one giant ball of knots. That's when.

Skimming my hand down her back, I try to pull out a few second-nature moves in the hopes of finding some sense of normal, but she tenses beneath my touch.

Fuck. We have to talk about how I left things.

"Hey, lil mouse." I soften my voice, aware we're in a crowded room but knowing we have to break this ice... even if it is in front of a bunch of people.

She glances my way and can obviously read the look on my face, because her expression buckles and she shakes her head. The look of pleading in her eyes is telling me she can't do this here, and I get that, but...

Shit, getting her to talk about how she feels has always been impossibly hard. Maybe I can take her—

Tink! Tink! Tink!

Asher taps his fork against his wineglass, grabbing the attention of the room.

"Speech!" Casey pumps his fist in the air. "Go, Bax-Man!"

Baxter cringes as we start to cheer. Mikayla grins, clapping loudly beside me. She's probably relieved by the distraction.

Bax clears his throat and looks down at Tammy. He holds her hand like he's drawing strength from her.

"I, uh…" He clears his throat again and checks his cards. "Thank you all for coming. Tammy and I are so happy you could make it."

"Finally!" Asher heckles him, and everyone starts to laugh.

"True. Looks like we're actually going to make it this time." His face lights with a grin. "Thanks for sticking with us. I love this beautiful woman beside me so much." He turns his smile to Kai and winks at him. "My family is the most important thing to me, and being able to make it all official tomorrow is something I've wanted for a long time now. We—"

A phone beside me starts ringing. It's on full fucking volume and draws the attention of the entire room. All eyes swing our way, and I glance at Mick, who is turning beet red.

"Shit," she mutters under her breath, digging it out, then wincing at the screen. Bolting out of her chair, she makes an escape out the side door, answering the call instead of ignoring it.

What the actual fuck?

I frown after her, reeling at the fact that she took the call during Baxter's speech.

Gritting my teeth, I sit back, my muscles tense as I listen to the rest of my friend's gushy tribute to his bride-to-be. I'm fuming by the time he's done, stalking out of the room to follow Mick while the guests applaud, then raise their glasses in a toast to the couple.

It doesn't take long to find my woman. She's pacing in the hallway, her heels digging into the rug and her ankle slightly twisting when she reaches the wall. With a huff, she pulls it off, dumping it down and hissing, "I told you I'm booked this weekend. You said it was okay. You signed off on this!"

My eyebrows wrinkle. I hate hearing her in distress. It makes me want to rip the phone out of her hand and yell at Ryan, tell him to fucking leave her alone.

"You did what?" she balks. "When?" She scoffs, like she can't believe what she's hearing. "You should have told me that!" Clenching her jaw, she listens to the rest of the call, pulling off her other shoe while sighing, "Yeah, yeah, I get it. Whatever it takes, right?"

I frown, not liking those words one bit. Hating the defeated slump of her shoulders.

Where's my fighter gone? Where's my Mick?

"I can't tomorrow... One of my best friends is getting married. I told you that... Can't they just delay?" She rolls her eyes. I'm pretty sure she's aware of me standing here but doesn't want to acknowledge that fact. "Yeah, I get it... Yes, I'm grateful. Thank you." She's saying it, but she isn't meaning it.

Her expression looks anything *but* grateful as her nostrils flare and she says a terse goodbye before hanging up.

"What was that about?"

She glances up but doesn't look me in the eye as she crosses her arms and shrugs. "Just a work thing."

"You look pretty pissed."

"Yeah, I just..." She holds up her phone, then sighs, rubbing her forehead and wincing.

"Mick, what did Ryan want this time?"

She blinks in surprise, but of course I know who she was talking to. Ryan is always calling her with bullshit tasks that she hates.

"He was just updating me on some changes to Axel's contract."

"The one he signed the other day?"

Mick nods, then mutters, "Apparently they made a couple changes to it while I was in the bathroom. Talking to you."

I can't help noting her slightly accusatory tone, and I frown at her. "What kind of changes?"

"Just an amendment that says I need to be present at a few events that Axel will be appearing at for this sponsorship thing."

"What?" I bark. "That's bullshit. They can't do that without telling you."

"Yeah, well, they did, and you know that I can't make a big fuss about it."

"Why not?"

"Because I have a performance review coming up. Because I could lose my job if I don't do what I'm told." She bulges her eyes at me like I'm stupid, and I can't contain this anymore.

"Then lose the fucking job!" I practically yell.

She bristles. "I've worked too hard to just walk away. Stop asking me to give up on my career."

"But this isn't the career you wanted," I practically whine, desperate for her to see this. How else can I word this shit to make her understand?

She lets out a patient sigh, although I can tell her insides are rippling with anger. That look on her face is lethal. Her voice is practically vibrating as she grits out, "I have to do the time. Ryan can help me get my career off the ground and give me opportunities that I won't find anywhere else. Yes, this job is stressful right now, but it will pay off." She tuts. "And I can't keep having this argument with you!" Her eyes flash at me like she wants to punch me in the balls and be done with it.

She wants to maim *me*—the guy who always has her back—and she wants to stick up for Ryan—the asshole who has no respect for her time and talent and...

I step back from her, shaking my head with a broken whisper. "I don't even know who you are anymore."

"What?" She blinks, looking slightly destroyed by my throwaway comment. But it's out there now, and I might as well keep going.

Softening my tone, I try to explain. "The girl I fell in love with would have told Ryan and his idiot athletes to stick it. She wouldn't just roll over and eat shit because they told her to. And she wouldn't have taken a phone call in the middle of someone's speech." I point behind me. "That's our family in there, and you were fucking rude."

She blinks at me, her face paling as she looks down at her phone, rubbing her thumb over the screen.

Guilt tears through me, and I try to gentle my voice even more. "I hate seeing you like this. Ever since you started this job, they've been chipping away at you. It's like you're losing yourself, and... I miss you. I want my wife back." My voice breaks and she glances up, staring at me with this expression I can't decipher.

"Uh..." Someone clears her throat behind me, and I whip around. Tammy gives me a gentle, apologetic smile. "Sorry to interrupt. I'm gonna take Kai home. And we just need to..." She points to the exit behind Mikayla, and we both step aside to let Tammy and her son pass.

He gives me a sad, wide-eyed look as he trails his mother, and all I can do is stare at him. My lips won't even pull into a smile.

The door creaks when they pull it open and Mick flinches, gripping her elbows, then dipping her chin when her phone starts ringing again. I stare at her, my expression silently begging her not to take it.

Her eyebrows bunch and she shakes her head, biting her lip before turning her back to me and answering the call.

All I can do is pivot on my heel and walk into the restaurant again, trying to put on a smile for my friends when all I feel like doing is smashing my fist through a wall.

CHAPTER 19
TAMMY

It's finally here. At one point, I seriously thought this day would never come. But Baxter's made it happen for us, and I'm fighting happy tears as I gaze at my reflection in the mirror. My original dress from three years ago still fits me perfectly. After Nova was born, I wasn't sure it ever would… but I've lost the weight I gained with her and am now back to my regular size. Brushing my hands down the dress, I swivel sideways and can't help an impish grin.

"I look pretty," I whisper, a thrill running through me when I think of the look on Baxter's face.

He still hasn't seen this dress. Lani's helped me keep it hidden, and I can't wait to see his eyes light with affection and that hint of awe he gets. Even after all this time, he still adores me, and I find it so incredibly humbling and thrilling. By the end of today, he's going to be my husband. I've never been so excited to do anything. This has been such a long time coming, and even as I lay in bed last night, listening to the steady fall of rain and worrying about how that will affect our day, I still couldn't squash the giddy lovebugs dancing in my chest.

Today, the minister is going to pronounce us husband and wife, and then we'll go and celebrate with our friends at some location that must be perfect by the excited little look Baxter's been getting on his face every time he says, "It's a surprise. Trust me, TT, you're going to love it."

"I am so here for all of it." I giggle the words, spinning like a little girl and loving the way my dress flares out.

The girls came shopping with me after Bax and I first got engaged and helped me design the perfect dress from all the things I saw and loved. The bodice is fitted and drops into a V that accentuates my breasts. Cinching in at the waist, it then falls to my knees. It's a unique wedding dress, but that's what I love about it. The skirt section is covered with a layer of glittery fabric that shimmers when I move, and it makes me want to spend my day spinning. My heels are tall and strappy, adding a few inches onto my short frame. Baxter won't have to bend down so far to kiss me.

"It's going to be perfect." I let out a soft squeal, then laugh at myself for acting like a child. But I can't help it! "I'm getting married today!"

The words pop out of me just as Lani and Rachel walk in the door, Nova toddling between them. Her hair has been curled, and she looks freaking adorable.

"Yay!" She raises her chubby little arms in the air, then barrels toward me. I crouch to greet her, hoping her hands aren't sticky.

"She's clean," Lani murmurs with a smile. "It's taken maximum effort, but between the two of us, we've kept her as pristine as we could."

I laugh, hugging my enthusiastic daughter, who is now jumping up and down, bashing my chin in her excitement. I lean away before she can do any more damage, grinning at her.

"You look very happy, my sweet."

She nods. "Me happy. You happy?"

"I am *so* happy."

With another cheer, she dances in a circle, then catches her reflection in the mirror and starts admiring herself. The dress we found for her is too cute. It matches the bridesmaids' outfits and makes her look like a princess—according to her. To me, she's a little cherub, and I adore her.

Brushing my fingers lightly over the top of her head, I then turn to my bridesmaids. "You both look so gorgeous."

Their cheeks bloom with color as they smile at me.

"Thank you so much for everything you've done. You truly are the bestest of friends."

I reach for their hands, and we stand in a circle.

"We love you. Being your friend is the easiest thing in the world." Rachel smiles, then pulls me into a hug. Lani gets in on the action, and we stand in a little circle while I soak up all the goodness that is this day.

"Oh, what time is it?" I pull out of the hug, glancing at the clock.

"Still ten minutes to go."

"Ugh. It feels like an eternity. I just want to get down that aisle and stand beside my man."

They laugh at my impatience, but I argue back that I've been waiting for this day for freaking *years*.

"Well, your wait is over, Tammy." Rachel takes my hand again, her smile glistening. "You deserve this special day."

"Thanks." I squeeze her hand and mouth, "Love you."

She grins and kisses my cheek just before my dad taps on the door and walks in.

"Ganpa!" Nova runs to him, and he swoops her up, perching her on his hip and telling her how pretty she looks.

I tense without meaning to. My parents always do that. As wonderful as they are with their grandchildren, they still make their own daughter feel like she's constantly letting them down.

But then he glances my way, and his eyes soften with a kind smile. "You look beautiful, Tamara."

"Thanks, Dad."

For a second, I think I see pride, but I glance away before I can overanalyze it. That look is so rare, I might just be imagining it.

"Right, only minutes to go." Lani claps her hands. "Let's get this show on the road."

"Is everyone seated in the chapel?" Rachel asks my father.

"Yes, all the guests seem to be here, and Baxter and the groomsmen are up front waiting for you."

A thrill races through me. "Okay, then."

I take Nova's hand once Dad's placed her on the floor beside me, and we head out to the entrance of the church.

Kai is waiting in his suit, looking very handsome, and my chest floods with affection.

"Wow," I murmur, tweaking his collar and brushing my hand down his jacket. "You look very grown-up."

"Thanks, Mom." His face is beaming. "You look pretty."

"Thank you, baby." I kiss his cheek, then quickly wipe the lipstick off before he complains. He follows it up by licking his finger and making sure his cheek is completely clean before handing Nova the basket of dried flower petals.

"You remember what to do?" He holds out his hand.

"Yep." She slips her little fingers into his, and I'm once again flooded with an overwhelming love for my children. Kai is so sweet with Nova, and she looks at him like he hung the moon.

"Here you go." Lani hands me my bouquet, then tweaks the fabric of my dress so it's sitting perfectly.

I thank her with a smile, then glance at the sound guy,

about to nod that he can start the music, but then my eye catches on something in the shadows of the entranceway.

Perched against the wall is...

"Caroline?" I whisper.

Rachel jerks to glance at me, then whips around, following my line of sight.

And sure enough, I'm right.

Caroline raises her hand in a feeble wave. "Sorry, guys. I know I'm supposed to be in there, but I just..." She shakes her head, still leaning against the wall and cast in shadow. "You go ahead without me. I'll watch from the back."

"Are you okay?" I let go of my father's arm and walk toward her.

"Yeah, I just needed to go to the bathroom and—" She hisses, her face bunching with pain as she rubs her belly.

Rachel and Lani are beside me in a second, studying Caroline as she battles a wave of pain and looks about ready to cry.

"Are you in labor?" Rachel whispers.

"No." She shakes her head. "I can't be. It's too soon. She's not due for another month," she squeaks, a look of panic washing over her face. "But something's definitely wrong."

"I'll go get Casey." I move toward the aisle.

"No!" Caroline tries to snatch my wrist. "This is your big day. I will *not* be the reason it doesn't happen for a third time. You have to get married. I'll be fine. Just—" Her expression buckles again, her mouth popping open as her body is gripped with obvious pain. She bends over with a soft moan, and I ignore all pleas to stay put, running down the aisle as a ripple of surprised whispers travels across our guests.

Baxter walks down the two steps to greet me, his face washing with concern.

"Baby, are you okay?" His big hand on my lower back is gentle and sweet, and I so wish I wasn't ruining this moment for him, but...

I look up at Casey, who is fighting a bemused grin at the way I just ran in here. But his humor quickly fades when I tell him, "Something's wrong with Caroline."

"What?" He jerks down the stairs.

"I think it's the baby."

The color drains from his cheeks as he chokes out, "Where is she?"

"In the entrance. She's in pain. We're not sure—" I don't even get to finish my sentence before he's bolting down the aisle.

Another ripple of whispers and shocked gasps cascades throughout the chapel as I share a worried frown with Asher and Bax.

Asher follows his friend, buttoning his jacket like a gentleman as he walks calmly down the aisle. I look up with an apologetic frown.

With a kind smile, Baxter brushes his fingers down my cheek. "You look so beautiful I want to cry."

I let out a soft, watery laugh, my eyes glistening.

"Happy wedding day." It's a feeble attempt at a joke, because we both know... this isn't happening right now.

He gives me a sad, pained smile and whispers a question he probably already knows the answer to. "What do you want to do, TT?

"I want to make sure Caroline's okay."

He nods, his smile tender as he takes my hand. "Let's get her to the hospital, then."

CHAPTER 20
CASEY

By the time I make it down the aisle, Nova is crying because she isn't getting to throw petals.

"They need to see my dwess!" she wails.

Aw, her pretty dress. I want to tell her she looks beautiful, but I can't form words. Not when I have *something's wrong with Caroline* ringing in my head. Fear grips me as I round the corner and spot her between Lani and Rachel. She's in obvious pain, and it rips my heart out.

"Baby?" I stop beside her, crouching low so I can brush the hair off her cheek and try to look at her face.

Her chin is dipped, and she's whimpering. "Something's wrong."

I fucking hate those words. It's an effort to keep my panic in check as I try to tell her that everything's going to be okay. But I don't fucking know! She lost a baby once, and there's no saying she won't lose another one.

Fuck, fuck, fuck!

"What's going on?" Ethan's deep voice makes me spin, and I spot him and Mikayla hovering behind us.

Asher appears a second later, and then Baxter and Tammy are walking into view, and I can breathe again. These guys will help me. My family's here. I can get through whatever shit this is.

"Liam's gone to get the car," Rachel murmurs. "Let's get her out front."

"We'll follow you," Ethan assures us.

"Dad, can you take Kai and Nova?" Tammy says.

"No," Caroline softly wails. "But your wedding."

"You are way more important than a ceremony." Baxter shakes his head. "Come on, let's get you to the hospital."

"But flowers, Mommy!" Nova starts crying again, and Baxter lifts her into his arms.

"You can throw those soon. We just need to make sure Aunt Caroline's okay first."

Nova's face bunches with worry as I walk past her, cradling Caroline against me. She's shuffling out of the church like a ninety-year-old, and after a few more slow steps, I can't take it anymore.

Lifting her into my arms, I carry her down the front steps. It's awkward with her big baby belly, and she's protesting that she's too heavy, but I ignore her, heading for Liam's waiting truck.

I'm nearly at the door when Caroline tenses in my arms, a cry punching out of her as she fists my shirt and tips her head forward.

"Is it like a contraction?" I ask, my voice rusty as I watch my wife in pain. It kills me every fucking time.

"Yes," she whimpers. "But it's too soon. She's not due for a month yet. We're not ready. What if something's wrong? What if she doesn't make it?"

The fear in her blue eyes renders me speechless. Thank fuck for Rachel, who opens the door and assures us, "She's going to make it."

Her quiet confidence takes the edge off my nerves as I place Caroline down, then help her into the truck.

She's crying unchecked tears as I close the door and buckle up, her chest punching with obvious panic.

"Just breathe." Rachel gets in the other side, stroking her hand and calmly talking her down. "Focus on your next breath. Think about only that. You can do this."

Liam drives at a decent clip but safely gets us to the hospital. Caroline's enduring another contraction as a nurse runs out the ER doors to assist us. She's brought a wheelchair and was obviously already prepped. One of the guys must have called ahead, and I'm so freaking grateful, I'm about ready to burst into tears myself.

I take Caroline's hand and she grips it like a vise, grinding the bones together while I clench my jaw and pretend it doesn't hurt.

The contraction passes as she slumps back in the chair, panting and already looking exhausted. I kiss the top of her head, and then the nurse starts wheeling her through the corridors with me walking alongside. This was so not the plan. That's going to be stressing Caroline out big-time. Her usual doctor isn't here, and the last time she was in this hospital, she was dealing with a miscarriage.

A shudder runs through me. I try to keep it on lockdown, not wanting to relive those memories of pacing the waiting room while she went into surgery. Her blood was all over my shirt, and I'd never been so scared in my life.

Although I'm pretty fucking scared right now.

What if we lose our little girl?

Shit, shit, shit! *Please don't let that happen*, I silently beg, forcing a smile when Caroline glances up at me.

Her big blue eyes are bright with fear, and as much as I'd like to join her, I have to be the strong one right now.

"In here." The nurse pushes Caroline into a room. "Let's get her set up on the bed. Dr. Bridges will be with us in just a minute."

The nurse works efficiently, helping Caroline into a hospital gown and checking her vitals before excusing herself to go find the doctor. The door clicks shut behind us, and we're suddenly swamped in silence. Our friends are no doubt pacing the waiting room, but it's just the two of us in here. Just me, needing to help my wife while I fight my own anxiety.

Caroline's breaths are shaky. She lets out another whimpering cry, and I perch on the edge of the bed, tucking her hair over her shoulder and brushing her tears away. "Baby, look at me."

Her eyes dart to mine, and I force what I hope is a calm smile.

"You got this. You're strong, and whatever we're facing right now, it's gonna be okay."

"I just don't want to lose her." Caroline cradles her stomach, and I rest my hand over hers.

"We won't." I don't know if that's true, but I'm fucking saying it anyway.

She sucks in a shuddering breath and holds it for a beat too long.

"Just breathe." I start rubbing her back. "It's gonna be okay."

Another contraction hits her just as the doctor walks into the room.

The man has a calm voice and a kind smile, but Caroline is still tense during his examination. I can sense she wants her own doctor—the smiley, cheerful lady with the reassuring brown gaze and sweet Indian accent. She's helped Caroline give birth to all our children, and now she's not here.

This man doesn't know Caroline's history. He doesn't know my wife at all, and it's obvious as he asks a plethora of questions that Caroline answers in terse, snappy beats. I end up taking over for her when she starts to cry.

The doctor seems unfazed by the emotion pumping through the room, and I rub my wife's hand and answer everything I can. She has to correct me twice, but we get there in the end—Caroline a blubbering mess and me barely keeping it together. I'm pretty sure my teeth will be ground to dust by the end of this.

"Well..." The doctor rips off his gloves, giving his

hands a wash while he informs us, "You're going into early labor. You're already six centimeters dilated, so we're in the active phase. By the sounds of your last birthing experience, we'll be meeting your little girl very soon."

"Will she be okay?" Caroline hiccups out the words. "She's not due for another four weeks."

His smile is soft, his voice reassuring. "Babies much younger than this have survived no problem. Her heartbeat is strong and steady, and her vitals seem good."

"But why is she coming early?"

"I'm not sure about that yet, but we'll monitor you carefully and do everything we possibly can to make sure you're all safe and well." Jotting down something on his iPad, he gives us one more smile. "I'll be back shortly to check on your progress. Try to relax as much as you can, and try not to worry. Focus on the fact that you'll get to hold your daughter soon."

The words settle into my chest, and my lips start to twitch. "Did you hear that, baby?" I turn to smile at her. "We're gonna get to meet our daughter today."

She sniffs and lets out a blubbering laugh. "We don't even have a name for her yet."

"That's okay." I kiss her forehead, then crouch down and brush my nose across her belly. "As soon as we see her, we'll know. Won't we, sweetheart?" I whisper against her bump, talking to our baby. "Can't wait to hold you, precious girl." Kissing Caroline's stomach, I then move up to her lips, cupping her cheeks and brushing my mouth against hers.

Her lips are wet and pliable, and I sweep my tongue against hers, kissing her deep for a brief moment before pulling back and gazing into her eyes.

"I love you. Having sex with you at that party and getting you accidentally pregnant was the best thing that ever happened to me."

She lets out a soft laugh and shakes her head.

"Falling in love with you was a no-brainer, and growing a family with you makes me so fucking happy."

Her blue eyes beam bright as she brushes her teeth across her bottom lip. "I love you too." She kisses me again and probably would have stayed against me if it weren't for another contraction.

"You know what I think it is?" I hold her hand and rub her shoulder as she battles a wave of pain. "She knows how awesome we are and just can't wait to meet us."

"Great," Caroline squeaks. "So she's as impatient as you and Billy are, then."

I laugh. "Probably."

She lets out a cry that turns into a watery laugh as she squeezes my hand and once again blows my mind with how amazing she is. The way she loves our boys... the way she's gonna love our little girl.

Damn, she's the best woman in the world... and I'm so fucking grateful that she's mine.

CHAPTER 21
BAXTER

Tammy's wedding dress billows out as she spins and starts pacing back toward me. Her heels click on the hard hospital floor, and I bounce Nova on my knee, trying to entertain her. She giggles, her curls bobbing while Kai starts playing peekaboo behind my shoulder. We've been in the waiting room for nearly two hours. Tammy's parents arrived with the kids forty minutes ago. Nova wouldn't nap and was turning into a "demon" child, according to Tammy's mother.

"She just wants her daddy." Mrs. Tan plopped her onto my lap with a small huff, then went to check on Tammy.

I couldn't hear their entire conversation, but the snippets I caught involved "wedding," "ruined," and "can't believe this is happening again!"

Her mother probably asked her if she's sure we're really meant to be together. In fact, I'm certain she did, because one: she asks that shit a lot, and two: Tammy's face went red, her nostrils flaring slightly as she hissed, "Of course it's meant to be. I've loved him most of my life, and he is going to be my husband! If it's not today, then it'll be another day!" Her hands flicked up, and everyone in the waiting room turned to look at her.

She caught my eye and I winked, my smile hopefully telling her how much I adore her. She grinned back, and then her mother huffed and sat down... and the pacing began.

I glance at Ethan and Mikayla. She's on her phone, tapping furiously while Ethan sits there with a mildly dark frown. Asher and Lani are whispering to each other, their fingers interlaced. He whispers something in her ear, and she giggles, nestling her forehead against his cheek and saying something back. Those two are seriously loved up at the moment. It makes me wonder what's going on with them. Is she pregnant or something?

"Again, Dada! Again!"

My thoughts are pulled back to Nova, and I grasp her little hands, neighing like a horse and giving her a bumpy ride on my knees before parting my legs and letting her flop into the space. She giggles like it's the funniest thing in the world, and I can't get enough of her dimples and her little teeth.

"Did we miss it? Is she okay?" Caroline's mother comes bursting through the door, Troy on her hip and Billy racing in behind them. Her husband follows with a stroller ladened with an overflowing diaper bag.

Nova jumps off my knee with an excited gasp. "Billy!"

She runs over to hug him, and they melt hearts before pulling apart and jumping around the waiting room together.

I go to stand, but Liam shakes his head at me and mouths, "I got this."

Moving closer to the toddlers, he stands watch, ready to jump in before they wreak too much havoc in this place.

"It's all good, Michelle." Asher stands, giving her a quick hug before kissing Troy's cheek, then wincing and wiping his mouth.

Lani hampers a giggle while she stands to greet them. "Last we heard, Caroline was doing great. We're due for another update very soon, so..."

Tammy stops beside me, her fingers twitching as she flicks them in the air. "I feel like it's taking forever. I just hope everything's okay."

"I'm sure it will be." Caroline's mother puts on a brave smile, rubbing Tammy's arm, then admiring her wedding dress before cringing. "Oh dear. It's happening again, isn't it?"

I take Tammy's hand, caressing my thumb across her wrist. She just nods and gives me a sad smile. Part of me wonders if I should have fought to just keep the wedding going, but there's no way Tammy would have been able to enjoy it knowing her friend was having a baby emergency.

"Dada!" Troy shouts, wriggling out of his grandmother's arms and shooting across the waiting room floor. He barrels into his father's arms. Casey's face is beaming as he scoops his kid up and then laughs when Billy wraps his arms around his leg.

"Daddy!"

"Unca Casey!" Nova grabs his other leg, and Casey lumbers across to us, smiling like he's just won a gold medal.

Kai runs over to give him some knuckles, his adoring smile making Casey seem like the freaking Pied Piper of Nolan. The kids giggle at their fun little ride on his legs, and Troy starts bouncing in his father's arms, scoring himself a raspberry on the neck. His laughter is infectious, and I can't help grinning at the adorable scene... and the look on Casey's face.

"How cute is his smile right now?" Mikayla murmurs with a soft laugh, then calls to him, "You got good news for us, man?"

"I have the best news!"

"So, she's okay?" Tammy asks.

"Caroline's doing great. She is currently holding our baby girl, getting in some cuddle time before she has to go into the incubator for a bit."

"The incubator?" Michelle covers her mouth with her hand as her husband steps up to wrap his arm around her shoulders.

"Yeah." Casey winces. "She's gonna need a little support to keep her body temperature stable, and she's got a touch of jaundice, but she's breathing okay, her heartbeat is strong, and the doctor assures me she's going to be absolutely fine." He nods, sucking in a relieved breath. "She's gonna make it."

"Oh, thank you, God," Caroline's mother whispers, closing her eyes and leaning against her husband's chest.

"When can we see her?" he asks.

"I know she's desperate to see all you guys, but I'm not allowed to send everyone through. Maybe you two could go first?" Casey points at his in-laws. "You might get to see her with the baby for a minute."

Her parents don't even wait a beat before they're rushing out of the waiting room and heading down the corridor.

"So, your baby got a name?" Ethan asks.

"She does." Casey grins. "I knew the second they put her against Caroline's chest. She looked up at me, and we both said..."

He looks between the boys, leaving us all in painful suspense until Lani huffs. "Just say it already."

With a soft laugh, he bounces Troy in his arms and says, "Lyla. Your little sister's name is Lyla."

"Lyla!" Billy shouts, testing it out.

"Lyla!" Nova copies him.

"Ly-ly-ly!" Troy claps his little hands.

I share a grin with Tammy while the rest of the adults laugh.

"That's really pretty," Rachel murmurs, crossing her arms and fighting obvious tears.

Liam tucks his arm around her waist and whispers something in her ear.

I glance back up at Casey and wonder why he's wincing at me.

"What?" I ask.

"We're really sorry about the timing on this thing. I feel like we ruined your wedding."

"Of course you didn't." Tammy brushes her hand through the air. "Nothing is ruined. The world has just gained a precious little girl. And I can't wait to meet her."

"Oh my gosh, she's so cute, you guys. She's got this red fuzz all over her head and these blue eyes and rosebud lips." His eyes get a little misty. "As soon as she's strong enough, you guys will be the first to meet her." He looks around the group. "She's adorable. My little Lyla."

And I get everything he's feeling right now. I have a stepson and a daughter, and I love them both equally, but there's something about being a girl daddy that's different. My protective instincts go into overdrive when I'm watching Nova, and I'm sure Casey will be just the same with his little Lyla.

"You know, out of all the ways our wedding has been postponed, this is by far the best," I tell him.

Casey laughs, setting Troy down when he starts to squirm. Liam steps away from Rachel, blocking Billy from taking off, while Ethan grabs up Troy before he can do a runner too. Nova skips across to me, and I pop her back onto my lap.

Now that we know everyone's okay, I'm thinking we should probably get out of here. As much as I want to see Caroline and Lyla with my own eyes, we can't crowd into a hospital room, and—

"Hey, guys." Caroline appears in a wheelchair, her father gently pushing her into the room. Her mother hovers nearby, obviously not loving the way her daughter is up and about.

I understand why. Caroline's face is pale, her smile weak and exhausted.

"Mommy!" The boys rush over to greet her, Troy trying to climb onto her lap.

Casey's eyebrows dip with concern as he moves back toward her. Scooping Troy up with one arm, he takes her hand and crouches down beside her. "What are you doing up?"

"Lyla fell asleep, so they took her to the incubator for a session, and..." She sniffs and shakes her head. "I can't sit in that hospital room alone when I know all my friends are waiting out here."

"You can, actually," her mother murmurs. "Everyone understands that you've just had a baby. They don't expect you to be out here visiting. This can wait, Caroline."

"It can't wait," Caroline insists, looking to her husband for support.

He gives her a soft smile and kisses her palm. "What's up, baby?"

"This has to happen today. We can't be the reason they don't get married."

My eyebrows dip together as I stand with Nova in my arms. "It's fine, really." I pull Tammy to my side. "You and Lyla are way more important."

She gives me a watery smile. "I can't wait for you to meet her." She lets out a soft breath. "I wish I had her in my arms right now, but I'm going to see her again right after this."

"After what?" Casey tucks a curl behind her ear.

"After Tammy and Baxter get married."

There's a thick beat of silence as we all throw her confused frowns.

She glances up at our faces and brushes a tear off her cheek. "I mean, it is ultimately up to you guys, and I know you're standing in a hospital waiting room right now, but all of our favorite people are here. It's Hockey House, you know?" She looks up at her father. "You're a minister. You could marry them right now, right?"

"Well, I..." He shares a soft look with his wife, who rolls her eyes but then ends up laughing and shaking her head.

"Oh, go ahead. You know you want to."

His smile grows, taking over his face as he glances at me. "I'd love to. I mean... it would be an honor."

Tammy lets out a surprised laugh, like she can't quite believe this, and I have no idea what to think. Exchanging vows in a hospital isn't exactly romantic.

"Do you... want to?" I give her an uncertain frown, but her smile is radiant as she nods.

"I want to be your wife. Let's just do it. Right here. Right now."

CHAPTER 22
TAMMY

A ripple of excitement shimmies through my chest as Baxter takes my hands and faces me. Our friends form a circle around us to try and block out the noises of the waiting room—the curious whispers, the nosy looks, the ring of the siren, and the bustle of the medical staff.

My mother stats muttering about how inappropriate this all is, but then my dad shushes her.

"Let them have their moment, Faith. Your daughter looks radiant. Enjoy this."

Mom shuts up, giving me a closed-mouth smile that I only barely see from the corner of my eye.

I'm focused on Baxter. On the tall, strong man in front of me. My best friend. The love of my life.

Nova tries to wiggle between us, and Rachel takes her, distracting her with soft tickles as Caroline's father clears his throat and begins a short service.

"We're gathered here today..." His words become muffled, turning to white noise as my world is consumed with Baxter. I drink him in, loving him with my gaze, my smile, a squeeze of my fingers.

He looks down at me like I'm precious. I'm the most beautiful woman in the world to him, and I can feel it all the way to my core. He loves me. He's only ever wanted me... and he's loved my son like he was his own... and now we have a daughter together. No matter what comes our way, I know we're going to last. We'll grow old and gray together. We'll never stop laughing and playing games and being each other's best friends.

"I love you," I whisper under my breath, emotion cutting my voice off.

Mr. Mason pauses, his smile kind and patient, before asking, "Do you have vows you'd like to exchange?"

"Yes." Baxter clears his throat, reaching into his pocket and pulling out a crumpled piece of paper. "I was going to try memorizing it, but I had no chance of pulling that off."

Asher gently snickers behind him, squeezing his shoulder, while Caroline shifts in her wheelchair.

She's probably sore and uncomfortable. She should be lying down. I glance at her, about to say it, but her smile is so full of joy. Everyone around us is insanely happy, and I can't stop this moment.

"Tammy." Baxter steals my attention, and the world turns fuzzy around me again. "I've loved you since the fifth grade. You're my best friend, and doing life with you makes me so incredibly happy. It's such an honor to become your husband, and I promise to love you and cherish you and look after you, through every up and down, for as long as I live. I will never judge you, I will never criticize you, and I will always protect you and cheer you on. I'll be honest with you, and I won't hide away, even when life gets hard. I'll be open with you, and I'll see you... every day, I'll see you."

It's impossible to hold back my tears, his rich voice filling me from the tips of my toes to the ends of my hair. My body buzzes, my heart thumping wildly.

"I'll love our children with everything I've got, and we'll raise them as a team. You are the only person I want do to do this with. You're my one, Tammy Tan, and you have my heart forever."

I hear a swooning sigh behind me, but I don't know who it's from. I can't take my eyes off Bax as I squeeze his hands and attempt to remember the vows I wrote three weeks ago.

My throat swells with emotion as I battle my tears, sniffing and willing my brain to comply. I spent hours memorizing those words, and they've all just disappeared suddenly.

"It's okay." Baxter brushes his thumb down my cheek. "Just say what you feel."

"What I feel?" I let out a soft laugh. "I feel so full of love for you. You are the best man I know. I love being with you, talking to you about anything and everything. I love that you listen. You actually listen, and you hear what I'm trying to say. You understand me like no one else does, and I love that so much." I blink, sniffling as I try to get this out. Kai's little hand rubs my arm, and I give him a watery smile before looking back up at Baxter. "You're my best friend, and I am so stoked that I get to be your wife. I will love you always. I will turn to you when I need help, and I will walk with you through any valley. I will hold your hand on the bad days when you just need to be quiet, and I will sing and cheer with you when it's time to dance and celebrate. I will be your partner, your teammate in all things—from parenting our beautiful children to shuffling through a retirement home with a walking stick. It's you and me forever, Baxter Brown, and I wouldn't have it any other way."

His eyes are glistening by the time I'm done. In fact, I'm pretty sure there's not a dry eye in this waiting room. Those close enough to hear us are wiping their cheeks with sappy smiles, and I can't help a soft laugh.

"Beautiful," Mr. Mason murmurs. "Now to the formal stuff. Baxter Brown, do you take Tamara Tan to be your lawfully wedded wife?"

"I do."

"And Tamara Tan, do you take Baxter Brown to be your lawfully wedded husband?"

"I do," I squeak, stars bursting through me as I let out a soft squeal and wiggle my hips.

"Yay, Mama!" Nova claps her little hands.

"Do we have the rings?"

"Yes." Kai steps forward, carefully taking a small pouch from his pocket.

With shaking hands, Baxter slips the ring on my finger. My hands are so tiny compared to his, and I love that about him. He's so strong and sure, and I know he'll stay true to his vows.

I feel so incredibly loved already, and I believe that's only going to get stronger as we live our lives together.

Slipping the ring onto his finger, I give it a squeeze and open my mouth with an excited smile.

"It is with great pleasure that, by the power invested in me, I can now pronounce you husband and wife."

A cheer goes up around us.

"You may now kiss your bride."

Baxter's arms curl around my waist as he bends down to meet my lips. I giggle against his mouth before he deepens the kiss, lifting me off my feet and holding me close.

"I love you so much," he murmurs between kisses.

"I love *you* so much," I whisper back, my insides going crazy when he pops me back on me feet and I stare at my wedding ring. "We did it!"

"About time!" Kai groans, and we all start to laugh.

This moment right here couldn't be more perfect. Sure, we're in a hospital waiting room and Caroline's in a wheelchair and her precious daughter is in an incubator, but I'm so freaking happy right now.

"Thank you." I take Caroline's hand, kissing her on

the cheek before Casey wheels her away to go see Lyla. Troy gets buckled into the stroller while Billy dances over seats, being chased by his grandfather.

Nova reaches for Baxter, and he nestles her in his arms as Kai wraps me in a hug. I kiss his head and snuggle him against me. We get a string of congratulations from all our friends... and those sitting around us.

"You know, the reception area is still set up. We could go there?" Lani suggests.

I look up to Baxter, to see what he thinks, and he's nodding in agreement. With broad smiles, we gather the tribe and start heading for the door and this special surprise he's planned for me.

Just as we're exiting the hospital, a cell phone rings behind me. I look over my shoulder, watching Mikayla wince, glance at Ethan, who's shaking his head, then answer the call.

"Fuck," he mutters under his breath, scowling deeply as she turns her back to him and walks around the corner of the hospital.

Running a hand through his hair, he stands there fuming while Rachel gives him a confused frown but is beckoned away by Liam.

I wonder if this has something to do with their fight last night, but it's probably not my place to ask. Slipping into Baxter's truck, I watch Ethan pace around the side of the building and hope everything's okay.

Baxter made some comment about Ethan and

Mikayla going through a few struggles at the moment. But surely they'll be okay. They're Ethan and Mikayla. They're one of my favorite couples ever. Their marriage can't be falling apart. They're meant to be together for life... just like me and Bax.

CHAPTER 23
ETHAN

"What is it now?" I bark as soon as she ends her call.

She jolts, obviously not realizing I followed her around the corner. I want to rip that cell phone out of her hands and smash it. She's been on it all fucking day. She even replied to a text during Tammy's vows, for fuck's sake.

Her shoulders slump as she takes in my expression, and her eyes dart to the ground. It's so obvious she's steeling herself, and my heart sinks. Raising her chin, she sniffs and tells me, "I have to go do this thing. I've been trying to get out of it all day, but they won't stop harassing me, so I need to just leave and get it done."

"In the middle of a wedding?" I flick my arms wide.

"The wedding's over now."

"What about the reception?"

She sighs, closing her eyes and squeezing the bridge of her nose. "I have to go, Ethan. It's in the contract, and

I'll get fired if I don't show. Shit, I could get sued if I don't go!" Her arm slaps against her leg, the shimmery fabric of her dress wrinkling.

She straightens it, pulling it back down her hips with a huff.

I want to tell her she can't do this. I want to drop to my knees and fucking beg her to stay, but we can't keep having this same conversation, right? She said so herself.

With a sad frown, I stare at my girl, wondering where she's gone, if my lil' mouse is even still in there.

Crossing her arms, she swallows and pulls her shoulders back, like she's preparing herself for some kind of verbal attack.

But all I can do is shake my head and murmur, "I can't keep going like this."

Her eyes dart to mine, her face the picture of devastation. I don't know why those words popped out of me, but they're true. I can't. I can't keep fighting with her over this fucking job. I can't keep watching her walk away from me.

So, for once, I turn my back and walk away from her first.

Running to catch up with Asher's car, I jump in the back seat.

"Where's Mikayla?" Lani asks.

"She's not coming. She has to work," I mutter, clenching my jaw as she exchanges a worried frown with Asher.

Thankfully, they don't say anything, and we drive to the reception in icy silence.

Fuck. I hate this so much.

The look on Mikayla's face just before I walked away is killing me, but when I turn to see if she's still standing by the hospital, she's not. She's gone. She will have jumped in her car and be heading back down to Denver by now.

Fuck. Fuck. FUCK!

Have I just lost my wife?

I think I might throw up and grit my teeth, having to concentrate hard around each corner as Asher heads to the reception.

The glade we decorated yesterday is now shimmering with lights, and wedding guests are milling around. We arrive in time to hear the cheer going up as Baxter and Tammy walk hand in hand into the forest area.

Tammy's gushing about how amazing everything looks, hugging Baxter and jumping in excitement.

"This is perfect!"

"Boo, you are a queen." Asher wraps his arm around Lani's waist and pulls her close. "You made this happen for them, and I'm so fucking proud of you."

She grins. "Thanks, baby." Holding his face with her thumb and forefinger, she pulls him in for a kiss, and I step around them before I seriously do start hurling chunks.

Everyone's asking how Caroline and the baby are. I listen to my friends give reports, then try to smile at people's delighted laughter over the fact that Tammy and Baxter got married in the waiting room.

People don't seem to mind that they missed it and are making the most of celebrating now.

But I can't fucking celebrate.

Mick should be here.

She shouldn't have chosen work over this.

She—

"Where's Mikayla?" Rachel stands in front of me.

I glance up from the picnic table I'm perched on, letting out a derisive snort. "Where do you think?"

Her eyebrows dip, and she smooths her bridesmaid's dress under her legs, taking a seat beside me. "What happened?"

"She got a call saying she had to be... I don't even know where the fuck she is, but she's gone there so she doesn't lose her shitty job. Some contract bullshit, and this guy called Axel or something is insisting she be there or the sponsorship deal with fall through. I don't know all the details." I huff, working my jaw to the side and wondering why Rachel is suddenly glaring at me.

Fuck, she looks like she wants to slap me right now.

"What?"

"You don't know all the details?"

I shake my head. "No."

"Why not?"

"Because I..." A breath whooshes out of me. *Because I didn't ask. Because I was too busy yelling at her for being a lousy, rude friend.*

"Ethan, why the hell are you sitting here sulking?"

I frown, not wanting to look at her as I pick at an invisible speck on my pants.

"Why didn't you offer to drive her?" Her voice gets a touch sharper, and I sit back, surprised by Rachel's aggravation. She's usually super chill and sweet, but I can sense her about to rip into me. "You should have gone with her. Axel's an ass. She told me all about him. And I know she's tough enough to handle him, but still... it's stressful for her. And now she's dealing with the stress of knowing you're pissed off as well."

Running my hand through my hair, I cringe, hating this lecture but not having it in me to walk away from it.

"You know, she has always supported your career. She's never once complained about all those times you're away. You have no idea how much she misses you, do you?"

I swallow, daring to glance at Rachel. She gives me a pained frown.

"She pined for you when you moved to Centennial, but she refused to let you see that because she didn't want you torn between her and something you love." She huffs. "And the number of games she made the effort to go to, even when she got slammed on social media for not being pretty enough for you."

"She's gorgeous," I argue. "Fuck those trolls. And I told them that."

Rachel closes her eyes, looking sad as she pats my arm. "Why aren't you supporting her through this the way she's always supported you?"

"I've been trying." My voice sounds feeble and small. "She needs to quit this job. It's bringing out the worst in her, and I'm desperate to make her see that, but she won't let me. How do I make her understand? She hates this job."

"Yeah." Rachel nods with a sigh. "But you know how sometimes you have to figure stuff out on your own? Mikayla is stubborn, and she's fiercely independent. She hates asking for help."

I scoff, knowing it all too well.

"And she hates being bossed around."

"Which is why this job is killing her," I grit out.

"And it's why her husband shouldn't be doing the same thing."

Guilt swamps me and I clench my jaw, fisting my fingers and wanting to fucking run from this conversation.

Rachel's gentle hand on my arm keeps me still. "Mick will figure it out. Right now, she's just afraid that she's not good enough to find what she really wants. She's worried that she's not smart enough to handle law school. She's afraid that if she leaves this job, she'll never get another chance again. She doesn't realize yet how truly brilliant she is and that there are so many pathways to get to where she wants to be." Her lips tip up in a sad smile. "You need to be there for her. She can't hear your logic when you're complaining. She's feeling torn, and it's eating her up. I can tell. Don't make things worse."

"I don't know what to do," I rasp. "I don't know how to

help her." My voice breaks, emotion taking me out on all sides until I feel like I'm about to cry.

"You could always start with 'What do you need, Mick?' or 'How can I best help you through this?' or 'Wow, you're so amazing the way you work so hard.' That kinda thing."

My insides buckle, regret pounding me like a battering ram.

Am I too fucking late?

"I don't know where she's gone," I rasp.

"So, call her. Ask. Find out."

Ripping the phone from my pocket, I dial her number, but she doesn't answer me. I try again, but it goes directly to voicemail, which means she's intentionally ignoring my calls. So, I text.

We need to talk. Please call me back, okay?

The message is instantly read, but she doesn't reply. I wait a full ten minutes, but she gives me nothing.

Sitting back with a helpless sigh, I show the screen to Rachel. Her crumpled expression is killing me, and I look away from it, feeling like the lowest form of scum possible.

God, please tell me I haven't just lost the best thing that ever happened to me.

CHAPTER 24
MIKAYLA

Ethan's words keep ringing in my head, and my hands won't stop shaking. Thanks to an accident and heavy traffic, it's taken me hours to get to this stupid presentation. I don't even know why I need to be there. Axel's such a douche. He added that stuff to his contract to mess with me. And Ryan, of course, put it in, no questions asked, because he wanted this deal to go through. He'll get bank from this, and what will I get?

You'll get nothing... and you'll lose your husband.

"*I can't keep going like this.*" Ethan's voice echoes through the back of my mind. Is he saying we should break up? Is he leaving me?

The blood in my veins has been replaced with ice.

"*I don't know who you are anymore.*"

His words keep tormenting me. Have I really changed that much? I didn't mean to. I've just been trying to do a good job. I can't succeed in this business unless I do my time, and being an assistant to this shit-stick is going to look great on my résumé. When I leave, he'll give me a great recommendation and—

Will he, though?

Or will he punish you for daring to leave?

Didn't he joke the other day that I'm his favorite lackey?

Asshole.

My shoulders twitch as I pull the door open and clip into the building. I'm still in my stupid wedding attire, the dress feeling out of place. I pull it down again, smoothing the fabric over my hips.

Cameras are clicking, people shouting Axel's name while the sponsors flap about excitedly, making sure their products are at the best angles in the background... and forefront... and the edges. Fuck, their shit is everywhere.

It looks ridiculous. Talk about overkill.

"We need to get on with this. Axel, can you turn around and smile at the cameras?"

"I'm waiting for my agent," he grumbles.

"I'm right here." Ryan waves with a cheesy smile.

Axel rolls his eyes. "I mean the pretty one. Need me some eye candy at this thing."

I stutter to a stop, knowing he's talking about me. Hating that I'm even here when I could be at a wedding reception with my friends and husband. The people I love and admire. The people who make me happy.

Happy? When was the last time you've been happy?

My stomach drops, Ethan's words ringing through me yet again. *"I don't know who you are anymore."*

Shit. He's so fucking right.

I have changed. I've lost my spark. My mojo. I'm just Ryan's disgruntled lackey, a hamster spinning a wheel and getting nowhere. But I've been too caught up to realize it. And now I'm about to lose my husband... for what?

"Mikayla!" Ryan notices me, beckoning me over with his fingers. "Finally! Took you long enough."

"There was an accident," I mumble, shuffling toward him. "Traffic was a bitch."

"Whatever, just—" He frowns down at me. "What are you wearing?"

"I left a wedding to be here," I snip. "I didn't have time to get changed."

His eyebrows flicker with some kind of emotion. I don't know what it is, but it feels negative, and I want to go back to Nolan so fucking badly right now.

"Hey, sexy lady," Axel sings as he flounces over to me, laughing in triumph. "Fuck, girl. You look hot."

My insides writhe as I cross my arms, forcing a smile and reminding myself that I'm contractually obligated to be here.

"What do you need me to do?" I try to put on my best professional voice, but I'm sounding small and mousy, which is so not me.

I might be Ethan's lil' mouse, but I am not mousy. I'm

strong and can speak my mind. I don't kowtow to assholes. That's one of the things Ethan loves about me.

But I've been giving in left and right, dropping everything to be here for these douchebags!

What the fuck is wrong with me?

"Okay." Axel grabs my hands, holding my arms wide and checking me out. His smirk makes my skin crawl. "You are so fine. We're gonna look great together." He gives my hand a little squeeze, then notices my wedding and engagement rings. "What are these?" He frowns. "Don't need those for the photo shoot." He pulls them off before I can stop him.

"What the fuck are you doing?" I snap, trying to grab them back.

He winces and glances over his shoulder at the curious crowd impatiently waiting for us. "Shhh. Chill. I'll give them back after we're done."

Gliding his hand around my waist, he steers me toward the cameras.

I tense, resisting him. "What are you doing?"

"I thought we could get some photos together."

"Why?"

"Because I want you beside me. You look so fucking hot, seriously. This is going to be epic. It'll boost my social media. I've already talked to the sponsors, and they're all over it. You'll help my image."

I wiggle out of his embrace. "I'm not your girlfriend. I'm married." I hold out my hand. "Now give me back my rings."

"He will." Ryan rolls his eyes, flicking his fingers. "Here, give them to me. I'll look after them, you'll take some pics, and then we're done."

Axel plops the rings into Ryan's palm with a huff, then gives me a pointed look. "It's in the contract, sweets. I want to be photographed with my agent."

"I'm not your agent." I rest my fist on my hip. "Ryan's your agent. I'm just his assistant. If you two want to get photos together, then you go ahead. I'm still trying to work out why the fuck I'm here."

"Because it's in the contract." Ryan glares at me, his eyes bright with warning as he obviously tries to keep his temper in check. "This will be a boost for the agency, seeing how great we are with our athletes, how we're willing to do anything to assist their careers."

"How is standing in a photo shoot assisting his career?"

"It gets him noticed, makes him popular with the public. You two look adorable together. It benefits everyone."

"Not me!" I yell, my voice ringing out. Cameras spin to face us, and I don't even care.

Axel looks over his shoulder and puts on a cheesy smile. "Can you guys give us a minute?"

"We've been waiting for hours! Can we get this done already!" someone complains from the back.

"One second." Ryan holds up his finger, looking just as cheesy as his prized athlete.

They both turn back to me with impatient scowls.

I glare right back. "You changed the contract without my knowledge and then signed it. I'm pretty sure that's illegal."

Ryan huffs. "You get your ass up there and smile for the cameras. We'll deal with this later."

"Yeah, come on." Axel steps into my space again, gliding his hand around me and pulling me close.

I slap my hands on his chest, pushing back... and all I can see is the empty space on my finger where my rings should be.

With a growl, I give him a hard shove, and my unexpected strength takes him off guard. He stutters back, only just catching his balance.

His face morphs into an angry scowl. "What the fuck is your problem?"

"You are," I seethe, then turn to Ryan. "And so are you!"

He bulges his eyes at me, snatching my arm and pulling me close. "What are you doing? Stop embarrassing us. You want to lose your job?"

I glare up at him, anger firing through me as I try to wrench my arm out of his grasp. He squeezes harder, and I wince at the pain.

"Let me go," I grit out, yanking against him.

"You are not leaving here. You are going to stand with Axel and smile and play nice, because if you don't, he's going to be a little bitch and make my life hell." His grip gets tighter with each sentence until the pain is radiating right to my bone.

I clench my jaw, using my other hand to pry his fingers off me. He finally lets go, and I snatch his wrist, forcing his hand open and retrieving my rings.

My insides are trembling with a mixture of rage and fear as I fist the diamond Ethan gave me and point up at my boss. "I quit."

"What?" He gapes at me like I've lost my mind.

"I..." I lick my lips and make sure my voice is ringing loud and clear. "Quit. I quit. I don't need this bullshit. You are a terrible boss, and I deserve better than this."

He pins me with an incredulous look, his cheeks going red before he whisper-barks, "Are you fucking out of your mind? If you walk away right now, you will *never* get another job with an agency again. I'll make sure of it. You think I don't have sway in this city? Your name is in Axel's contract. You better do what it says, or I am suing your ass, do you understand me?"

I shake my head, stumbling back from him. Axel tries to steady me, but I flick him off. "Fuck you." I frown at him. "Fuck you both. I don't need this shit."

Spinning on my heel, I fist my rings so hard, the diamond starts cutting into my palm. Clipping out of the building, I race to my car and slam myself inside it.

Ryan runs after me, and I start the engine and punch the gas, screeching away from him before these silent sobs start jerking my stomach.

Shit. I cover my mouth with my hand, whimpering into the back of it as tears roll down my cheeks.

I hate crying.

I don't do tears.

But it's like a fire hydrant has just exploded inside me. I pull over on a quiet street and park beside the curb. Gripping the wheel, I let go, sobs punching out of me as I finally release all the shit that's been festering for months.

I don't know how long I sit here for, and I have no idea why I'm even crying by the end of it.

So much regret and pain is swirling through me, I can't even figure out what is hurting the most.

I feel like shit. I just want to go home.

I want Ethan.

Glancing into the passenger seat, I stare down at the rings he gave me. I pick them up and try to slide them back on, but my fingers are shaking too badly. Dropping them, I rest my head back against the seat and close my eyes.

I should call him, tell him what happened.

But I don't even have the energy to reach for my phone.

I ignored him before. Ignored his text because I couldn't talk about what he'd said... or the fact that I'd just walked away after he said it.

Is it more than just my job that's killing us?

Are we heading for the end no matter what?

The thought hurts more than I can fathom. I press my hand into my belly, aching in my core. The pain spreads through my body, and a fresh wave of tears takes me out.

"I love you," I whisper to Ethan, even though he can't hear me. "I don't want to lose you."

Gazing down at my ring finger, I brush my hand over the spot where my rings should be. My annoying big rings that always get in the way, that can be ripped off my finger so easily.

I can feel my eyebrows dipping as I relive that moment Axel stripped me of them. A shudder runs down my spine, and then I ping straight, an idea hitting me with a force so strong, I start the engine.

Snatching my phone, I do some quick research and am soon pulling up outside a tattoo parlor.

Yes, I'm being impulsive, but this feels so right that I don't have any other choice.

I'm married, dammit, and the whole fucking world is going to know it—every damn moment of every single day.

CHAPTER 25
ASHER

We woke late thanks to not falling into bed until three in the morning. The wedding reception was awesome. The weather held out, and we partied late into the night. Champagne flowed, the food was delicious, the speeches were funny, and people started heading home around one. Baxter and Tammy floated out of there, driving off to some unknown destination to have a few nights just the two of them. I'm sure it'll be filled with sex and sleep and all things good.

After they left, we finished cleaning up with a grumpy-ass Ethan, who barely said three words the whole night, and an actually helpful Rachel and Liam. Thank fuck Ethan decided to bug out early. I offered to let him crash on the couch, but he said he wanted to go home. He looked damn miserable when he said it, and we spent the first hour of cleanup detail worrying about Ethan and Mikayla.

It made me grateful that my relationship with Lani is so solid. And it made me realize how much I want to marry her and be with her for the rest of my life.

When we finally crept up to the top floor of the villa, I was exhausted but so loved up that I had to peel Lani's clothes off and make her come. She was up for it, and feeling her shudder and writhe beneath me was heavenly. She came as I licked her sweet pussy and then came again when I buried my cock inside her. I'm never gonna get tired of her luscious curves and sexy body. Even if it changes with age, I'll love every version of her, because when I'm inside her that way, we're connected on a spiritual level. I don't care if I get shit for saying stuff like that, because it's the truth. This woman owns me—body, mind, and *soul.*

Her soft sigh against my chest makes me smile. I cup the back of her head, lightly playing with her thick curls as her naked boobs press against my bare torso. I fucking love being naked with this woman. We have nothing on today, and spending it in bed, watching Harry Potter for the gazillionth time (like we're doing right now) sounds like an awesome use of our time. I wouldn't mind going down on her again too... and whatever else that might lead to.

No clothes. No schedule. No pressure.

Pure perfection.

Skimming the pads of my fingers across her shoulders, I press my lips to her forehead and notice a slight tension in her muscles. I start to knead her neck, and she sighs again, her moan soft and pleasurable.

"Want a massage, boo? Here, lie down."

"No, I'm okay. This is good," she murmurs, draping her arm across my waist. Her sapphire ring glints in the light, and I smile, brushing my thumb over it before looking back at the screen.

Harry casts a spell on Snape, who goes flying back and crashes into an old bed. Ron and Hermione are horrified, and all I can think about is why my woman isn't feeling as relaxed as I am.

I rest my cheek against her forehead. "You tired from last night?"

"Yeah." She yawns. "It all worked out in the end. Thank God. When we had to go to the hospital, I was like 'you've got to be kidding me.' Poor Caroline. Poor Bax and Tammy. I so didn't want them missing out again."

"I know, right?"

"But they didn't. And all our efforts on the reception weren't wasted either." She looks up with a smile. "Thanks for helping me."

"Always. We're a team."

Her smile turns mushy, so I peck her lips, the idea of doing more running through me. I skim my fingers down her back and am seconds away from rolling her over and covering her with my body when she lets out another sigh.

"Okay, what's the matter?"

"Nothing."

I nudge her off me, spinning in the bed so I can hold her face and narrow my eyes at her.

She blinks at me, her smile coy, and I shake my head with a smirk. "If you were wearing pants right now, they'd be on fire."

With a soft snicker, she rolls her eyes. "Okay, fine. I can't stop thinking about the wedding yesterday and how sweet and intimate and unorthodox it was. And then my mind starts swirling with how many times their plans got thwarted by life... because life can suck sometimes." She huffs, her face scrunching as she lifts her hand and gently plays with her ring. "And then I started thinking about how much I love this ring, and how my sisters are going to flip out when they see it and wedding plans will be fired at me left, right, and center. Plans that could fall to crap, and it'll be all pressure, and I'll be busy trying to please everybody and put on the best damn day possible and..." Her shoulders slump. "What should be a special, intimate thing for you and me will become this huge event for everybody else." She shakes her head. "It makes me not want to go through with it."

"What?" I choke out the word, my heart spasming. "No, you gotta marry me. You said yes, woman."

She smiles, cupping my cheek. "I want to marry you, but I don't want a wedding." Her nose wrinkles. "I know Tammy and Baxter's big day would be considered a disaster. That's what people are going to say, but watching them get married in that hospital waiting room was perfect."

My eyebrows rise. "You want me to try and book out St. Vincent's Memorial?"

Laughter bubbles out of her as she gently rests her hand on my chest. Her painted nails lightly brush my pec before drawing a circle around my right nipple. "I guess part of the reason I've been so slow on this engagement thing is because I've been worried about the wedding. I kept putting you off because I don't want to have to deal with what comes next."

Brushing my thumb across her cheekbone, I thread my fingers behind her neck and pull her toward me. "C'mere."

She leans into my kiss, sinking against me and climbing onto my lap. Our torsos meld together, her perfect pussy nestling against me as I splay my hands across her back and look into her eyes.

"I get it, boo. My mom's going to be a nightmare. You didn't say it, but I know you were thinking it."

She blushes and dips her head. "We won't even recognize half the guests, will we?"

"Probably not." I tip my head... then go still, my lips parting.

"What?" She gives me an expectant look, those eyes I love so much bright with curiosity.

I drink her in, my smile growing as I thread my fingers through her hair. "Do you trust me?"

"Yes."

I love how she doesn't hesitate. I love the faith in her eyes.

And as much as I want to spend the day making love to this gorgeous woman, there's something I want to do even more.

"Get up." I nudge her off me, jumping out of bed and pulling clothes from my closet.

"Why?" She gives me a skeptical frown, reluctantly sliding to the edge of the bed.

Shoving my pants on, I rush to zip them and lift my chin toward her closet. "Come on. Get that cute ass out of bed."

"Where are we going?" Flicking the sheet off, she walks to the closet, and I'm numbed for just a moment by the mesmerizing sway of her hips. She's a goddess, and I have to force my gaze away, will my body to turn around, because sex can wait.

"Asher." She sings my name. "What is going on in that head of yours right now?"

I spin, walking across the room and pulling her into my arms. Lavishing her with a deep kiss, I then pull back, peck the end of her nose, and whisper, "Let me surprise you, boo. Please, just give me this one."

Her smile is stunning as she drinks in my expression and lets out a breathy laugh. "Okay, fine. I will let you surprise me this one time because the look on your face is so frickin' adorable."

"Thank you, baby." I kiss her again and practically

skip out of the room, heading to my office and grabbing everything we'll need to make this the best day ever.

I'm serious.

This is going to be the best day we have ever had together.

CHAPTER 26
LIAM

Working on a Sunday after being at a late-night wedding does not make me the nicest guy to be around. I'm normally calm and unflappable, but it's taking maximum effort to hide my mood this morning. I'm worried about Ethan and Mikayla. He looked like shit last night, and I didn't want him driving. He promised me he wasn't drunk, but I hadn't been keeping a close enough eye on him to know for sure. His breath didn't reek of alcohol, but I couldn't relax until I heard from him a few hours later.

Crashing at Dad's.

That's all he said, so then I tossed and turned, wondering why he hadn't gone home. It's obvious that his marriage is in trouble, but it's not over, right? Shit, that would break everyone's hearts. Mikayla and Ethan are endgame. If *they* can't make it, what chance do the rest of us have?

And that made me pull Rachel into my arms and hold her close while she slept. My touch stirred her, and she turned her head to kiss me, her ass nudging back and inviting me to wake her up with a little loving. I knew she was exhausted, so I kept it simple, sliding into her from behind while we lay on our sides. I caressed her body and enjoyed her reckless groaning, working her clit while I rode her. She orgasmed just before me, her inner walls clutching me until I spasmed inside her. She milked me dry, and we drifted right back to sleep, my hand tucked beneath her boob and her body secured against mine.

I can't lose her, but what I wouldn't give to have those times we make love result in something more. I wish I could give her everything she wants. Not that she'll be able to get that with another guy either. Her body doesn't seem capable of growing a baby, no matter how hard we try. It hurts me, too, but I get the feeling she's more heart-broken than I am. As long as we have each other, we'll be all right...

But what if I'm not enough?

You are.

And logically, I know this is true, but I'm not feeling it this morning, and it's making me a grumpy ass.

I just wish there was some way I could make this adoption thing happen faster. Rachel's ready for a kid now. *I'm* ready for a kid now. Watching Casey's face when he announced the birth of Lyla was golden. I want that. I want to be a daddy.

"Liam."

"What?" I bark, then instantly wince. "Sorry." I clear my throat and spin in my chair, trying to put on a smile. "What's up?"

Officer Reed stares at me, her eyes narrowing. "You okay?"

"Yep." I nod, trying to make my smile wider.

"All right, well..." She shakes her head, obviously not believing me as she walks over with a manila folder. "I just need you to double-check this accident report from Friday and sign it off for me."

"Oh, yeah." My stomach sinks, thinking about those poor kids. Social services came to collect them. The baby was sleeping, and the little boy had softened to quiet whimpers against my chest by the time the woman arrived. She was sweet and kind, coaxing Carlos into her car. He seemed scared, but I spoke to him in Spanish, assuring him everything would be okay.

Watching his little face peering through the glass with that worried frown was a killer. I just hope they can make it back to family soon. People they'll feel safe with. People who can help them heal.

"Do you know if they got hold of the family?" My pen scratches across the paper as I sign my name.

"Yeah, it's heartbreaking."

I pause, my pen frozen in midair as I forgo my next signature and glance at her. "What do you mean?"

"They've only got three grandparents and one uncle who all live in El Salvador. They don't want the kids back."

"What?" I rush my signature, botching it, before slapping the folder closed. "Why?"

"They insist they'll have a better life staying in America. Both kids were born here, so they're citizens, and the family doesn't want them being sent back home."

"So, what's going to happen to them?"

"They'll be placed in foster care."

"And that's better than being with family?" I balk.

"I know." She shrugs. "I can't decide how I feel about it. I mean, on the one hand, you're like 'come on, they're family,' you know. But then I guess you could be thinking, 'wow, what a huge sacrifice they're making for these kids.' They'll definitely have more opportunities here than there."

"Not if they're stuck in a foster system where they get bounced around."

"Well, the family is obviously hoping some lovely people will adopt them, but..." She shakes her head with a sad frown. "As we well know, that's not always the case." She sighs. "There are so many great foster parents out there, but there are also some horrible situations. It's so unsettling for little kids, you know? I just hope these two have a success story, especially with the trauma they've already faced. Whoever they end up with is going to be dealing with their pain. It's a big ask, but there are a lot of bighearted people out there, and we just have to hope these kids end up in a home that can nurture them, you know?"

Officer Reed tucks the folder under her arm and walks away from the desk I'm using. My heart is pounding for reasons I can't explain... until my slow-ass brain finally clicks. I snatch the phone off its charger.

Rachel answers after three rings. Her voice is quiet, and I can tell she's tired and probably feeling kind of melancholy after everything that happened yesterday. She would have given anything to be holding a precious little girl in her arms.

Well, maybe she can.

"Hola, cariño."

"Hey. How's your shift going?"

"Just paperwork at this stage. No emergency calls I've had to deal with, so that's great."

"Good."

Damn, I love her sweet voice so much.

My breath catches just before I blurt, "You know the accident I told you about? The one that made me late for the rehearsal dinner?"

"Yeah. There's an article about in the local paper. I was just reading it online. Those poor kids. Have you heard how they're doing?"

"Actually, that's why I'm calling. I haven't spoken to social services yet, but... how would you feel about a foster-care situation?"

She pauses, and I can picture her face. She's probably blinking while she thinks, or maybe brushing her bangs aside like she does when she knows she's going to say something I might disagree with. "I don't know, Liam. I'd much rather adopt, even if that means waiting longer. I just can't bear the thought of falling in love with kids I'll then have to lose or give back or say goodbye to."

I lick my lips, nodding my understanding. "Thing is, there's a chance this situation could turn into an adoption. The family is from El Salvador, and they're saying they don't want the kids sent back." I let out a soft sigh while Rachel gasps.

"They don't want them back? Why?"

"Right now, they're saying the kids have a better chance in the States. More opportunities, you know?"

"But... they need their family."

"I know." I nod, picking up my pen and tapping it on the desk. "Or they need *a* family. People who can love and care for them while they deal with their trauma."

Rachel doesn't say anything, and I let that thought sit for a minute.

"Ray, I think we should take these two. Even if the family changes their minds later, these kids need us right now, and that's more important than our fear of getting hurt down the line, you know? We can give them a safe home. A place to heal. We'd just have to take one day at a time."

Rachel's swallow is thick, followed by a trembling breath.

I grip the phone, pressing it to my ear while I give her

time to think this through. I'm just opening my mouth to say more, but she speaks before I can.

"Okay," she whispers. "Let's do it. If social services will let us, let's take them for as long as we can have them."

A rush of emotion swamps me as I suck in a breath and start to nod. "Okay. I'll call now."

"Okay." Her voice is soft and breathy, matching mine.

"I'll call you back as soon as I've spoken to them."

"Okay." She lets out a wispy laugh. "I'll just be the one pacing by the phone."

"I'll be as quick as I can."

"Uh-huh."

"Hey, Ray?"

"Yeah?"

I grin. "I love you."

I can picture her smile and swear I hear her teeth brushing over her bottom lip before she whispers, "I love you too. No matter what. Always."

"Always," I gently reply, then hang up to make the most important call of my life.

CHAPTER 27
ETHAN

Always. That's how long I thought my love with Mikayla would last.

I was convinced we were endgame, but when I got home last night, she wasn't there, and I couldn't be in our apartment without her. So, I headed to Dad's place and have spent the morning listening to him lecture me about the fact that Mikayla is the best thing that has ever happened to me, and I better not lose her.

So that was fun.

And it definitely helped me leave.

As much as I didn't want to walk back into an empty apartment again, I drove home.

I have no fucking idea where Mikayla is. I've tried calling her, but it just goes straight to voicemail, and the stream of texts I've sent her haven't even been read.

Fuck. I don't know if I should be scouring the city for

her or if she's holed up in some shitty motel room because I told her I was done.

Which I fucking didn't.

I told her I couldn't keep going like this.

Which she could have interpreted as done.

Shit, shit, fuck-balls!

"You asshole," I mutter to myself, clomping up the stairs and punching in our key code.

Shoving the door open with my shoulder, I slam it behind me and flinch when I see Mikayla sitting on the couch. Her legs are curled up like she's been hugging her knees. As I slowly walk down the short corridor, my steps loud on the polished floor, she unfurls herself and stands. She's so short, so petite, yet her size never made her weak or vulnerable.

She's normally feisty as hell. But right now, standing there in boxer shorts and one of my shirts, she looks tiny. My button-down engulfs her, swallowing her hands and slipping off one shoulder. She quickly pulls it back up and blinks at me.

Her eyes are wide and red around the edges. Has she been crying?

Fuck.

It takes a lot to make my woman cry, and I'm sure it's my fault that she's been curled up on our couch weeping. The image kills me. My chest constricts, guilt squeezing my insides to mush.

She sniffs, wiping her eyes before crossing her arms.

My lil' mouse.

My precious lil' mouse. I love her so fucking much.

I want to lift her against me and cradle her to my chest. I want to tell her I'm sorry for being an ass and that—

Wait. What the fuck?

My eyes narrow in on her arm. My shirt has slipped again, spilling over her shoulder, and that's when I see the purple bruises on her skin.

"Did someone hurt you?" I snap, growling my way to the couch and pulling the fabric down so I can get a good look at...

Finger marks.

Someone grabbed her. Squeezed her arm. Did he touch her anywhere else? Did he threaten her? Is this asshole the reason she's been crying?

Rage tears through me in a heat wave that I can't counter.

"It's fine," Mick mumbles, pulling away from me and tugging my shirt back up.

"It's *not* fine! Who did this to you? Was it Axel? I'm gonna end that motherfucker."

She closes her eyes. "No. It wasn't him."

"Then who? Where were you? What happened? Tell me exactly what happened!"

Letting out a soft sigh, she dips her head, and it's only then that I see how truly exhausted she is. She's pale and spent, gray smudges under her eyes, and I'm standing here like a complete douchebag, yelling at her.

Gripping my mouth, I take a small step back and fight

to keep my rage in check. I'm not angry with her; I'm livid with whoever left marks on her skin. But she's the one getting my fire. She doesn't deserve this shit, and I—

I huff, shaking my head and saying as softly as I can, "I'm quitting hockey. I'll call Coach and my agent tomorrow and let them know. Figure out the best way to get me out of my contract and—"

"What?" Her head snaps up. "You are *not* quitting hockey. Are you crazy? You have the potential to be one of the best players in the NHL. You can't give that up."

"I gotta do this."

"Why?" Her voice is high and incredulous.

My shoulders slump as I puff out the words. "To save my marriage. To protect my wife!"

The room goes still as she absorbs what I just said. I don't know how to fill this painful silence, so I just ride it out while she scratches the side of her nose, then shakes her head and finally huffs.

"You're not quitting hockey for me." She scrapes her fingers through her hair. "This isn't even a discussion, Ethan. No! I won't let you."

"Don't you get it?" I step in front of her before she can march around the couch and stomp up to our room. Bending down, I cup her cheeks and force her to look at me. "You mean more to me than hockey ever will."

Her eyes start to glisten. "But it's your passion."

"*You're* my passion, Mick!" I tap my chest, stepping back as these desperate words fly out of me. "Us. Together. That's what keeps me going!"

Her expression crumples like she's fighting tears, her voice wobbling. "You're not doing this."

"Yes, I am."

"No... I won't let you. It's your dream."

"And being an agent is yours," I argue. "I've had my time. It's your turn. I will drop everything, okay? I'll go to all your meetings and every event. Even if I just have to stand on the edge of the room and play bodyguard, that's what I'll do. Because no one gets to leave marks on my woman." My voice catches as I point at her arm, and holy fuck, now I'm fighting tears.

Emotions are raging through me in a torrent I can barely control. Seeing Mikayla hurt kills me. Watching her cry kills me. I need to be there for her. I should have been right from the start. I should have—

"That's really sweet, but..."

"But what? Why won't you let me try to fix this? I want to help you. Please don't push me away. Let me do this for you. For us. I can't... I can't lose you, Mick." Tears line my lashes, and I grimace, blinking away the blurry moisture, desperate to pull myself together.

I don't cry.

I'm strong.

I need to be strong for her.

She lets out a soft whimper and covers her mouth. I move to embrace her, but she holds up her hand and steps away from me.

It's crushing, brutal, and I can't wipe my own tears

away fast enough. A few pop free, and I let them trail down my cheeks.

"I haven't been living my dream life," she blubbers, tipping her head up to the ceiling. She closes her eyes, and for a second, I freak out that she's about to ask for a divorce or some shit. Maybe I used to be her dream, but I'm not anymore.

"Mikayla—" I breathe, but she cuts me off before I can say another word.

"I have desperately been trying to make my job everything I wanted, because I didn't think I could succeed without it. I thought I had to pay my dues, you know? Like I wasn't worth something better." She crosses her arms like she's trying to hold herself together. "But you were right. As much as I hate to say that... you were." Her laughter is short, watery, and borderline hysterical. "When we first met, I wanted to represent female athletes who weren't getting enough attention, not work my ass off for arrogant pricks and cocky, handsy athletes."

"Handsy?" I jerk up straight. "Did that Axel fuck touch you? You said it wasn't him. Did he try to do something and then grabbed you when you were getting away from him? What happened?" I snap, then suck in a breath and close my eyes. "Mick, I swear to God if he—"

"It wasn't him." Her voice cuts through my panic, then goes small. "It was Ryan. He got pissed with me when I told him exactly what I thought. He grabbed my arm and—"

I growl in my throat, my hands fisting at my sides.

"And I quit." She gives me a pointed look.

All the anger in me evaporates. Well, most of it. Surprise sweeps away the bulk of my wrath, leaving only small remnants that can come back to life after I've processed this unexpected news.

She sniffs. "Yeah, I quit. I broke my contract, and who knows what kind of shit that's gonna get me in, but I just couldn't be there." She shrugs. "So, I stormed out, and then..." She works her jaw to the side. "I went to my car and sobbed." Her face crumples, and I move toward her but am stopped when she raises her hand and blubbers, "And then I got a tattoo."

I stare at her ring finger, my breath on hold as I take in the delicate tattoo inked on her skin. It's a stylized *E* set in the middle of an infinity symbol. It's still raw and looks kind of painful, so I'm extra gentle as I take her fingers and fold them over mine.

She sniffs, her voice still quaking. "Just because I don't wear your ring doesn't mean I'm not constantly thinking about you. You're always with me, Ethan. And when we're not together, I miss you so much it hurts." Her voice catches, and I wrap my arm around her, pulling her to my side and kissing the top of her head.

"You quit your job and got a tattoo," I whisper into her hair, still reeling and now fighting this unexpected laughter bubbling in my chest.

She nods, her voice muffled by my sweater. "Felt really good, actually." Pulling away, she looks up at me with glassy eyes. "Not sure what I'm gonna do now, but...

I think I just need to be with you for a while. Even if that means following you around and becoming some heinous hockey wife."

"You'll never be heinous." I brush my knuckle down her nose. "But you'll always be my wife."

"Yeah, I will." Her eyes light with beauty, my heart stretching like it's taking its first full breath in months. "Like I'm gonna do life without you."

My smile grows with relief, and I can tell she's relieved, too, but there's still a touch of sadness lurking in her expression. The last twenty-four hours must have been total shit for her.

"I'm sorry I wasn't there," I rasp. "I should have driven you to Denver."

"It's okay." She shakes her head. "I needed to do this on my own anyway. And it probably wouldn't have looked great to have a pro hockey player arrested for beating the shit out of a sports agent, you know?" She wrinkles her nose in jest, and I mirror her expression, although my tone is serious.

"It's not okay what he did to you, and I want to break that piece of shit."

"But you won't." She pats my chest. "Because I need you here with me, not in jail. You've got your best season yet coming up."

"Do I?"

"Yeah, you didn't know that?" Her eyes start to sparkle with that playful look I first fell in love with.

I grin and press my lips to hers, pulling away only

long enough to promise, "We're gonna find a way that works for both of us, okay? I love you, and I want you to be living your best life. I want to help you make your dreams a reality."

She goes up on her tiptoes, squeezing the back of my neck. "*You're* my best life, and the rest I'm gonna figure out along the way. For now, I just want to be with you and wash away the shittiness that has been the last twenty-four hours."

My right eyebrow arches as I smirk. "Well, we better get in the shower, then."

CHAPTER 28
MIKAYLA

Ethan plucks me off the ground, and my legs automatically wrap around his waist. I kiss his cheeks as he carries me up the stairs. I've never seen him cry before, not even on our wedding day. But seeing those tears trail down his face as I stepped away from him was a revelation. I swear I've never loved him more than in that moment. His pain over the thought of losing me was so freaking humbling. He loves me. He was willing to quit hockey for me.

I've never felt so important to anyone in my life. I don't even know what to do with that. Trailing my fingers into the ends of his hair, I lightly play with them as I press my lips to his and drink in his taste, that familiar flavor of him.

How many times have we kissed in the past six years?

How many times has his tongue swept across mine?

Yet this time feels new, different somehow.

It's deep with meaning, like my soul is seeking out his, desperate to connect on a level we've never experienced before.

We reach the bathroom, and Ethan pops me down to turn on the shower.

I start unbuttoning his shirt—so big and cumbersome on me, but I love it just the same. He gently flicks my fingers away and takes over, delicately pushing each button through the hole until it's spread apart, my body on display. I didn't bother putting on a bra this morning. I got home so late last night, and Ethan wasn't here. I wept some more, pulling out his shirt and crying into it before putting it on and finding a perch on the couch. I barely slept. With the curtains open, I watched the sun lighten the sky while I sat on the couch and wondered where my husband was.

I could have called him, but I couldn't bring myself to turn my phone on. After the string of abusive texts from Ryan after I walked out of there, I switched it off. It was tempting to throw the thing in the trash can, but I kept it in my bag, buried deep and untouched.

Waiting for Ethan to return was pure torture.

But then he arrived.

And now he's standing in front of me, gazing at my naked body like he's in awe. Like he can't believe he's lucky enough to call me his.

Lifting my hand, he brushes his lips over my tattoo, smiling down at it and murmuring, "I really love this, you know? Think I might have to get myself an *M*."

I want to grin up at him, but emotions are still riding through me. I feel raw and fragile, so I step against him, rising to my tiptoes and kissing his lips again. I need this connection. I have to be with him. To seal this new start with a physical act. I can't talk anymore. There are no words, only hands and hearts and bodies.

Scrambling to pull his shirt off, I quickly unbuckle his belt. My movements turn frantic, a little whimper popping out of me.

"It's okay, lil' mouse. I'm not going anywhere."

Tears burn my eyes again, and I can't look up at him. Instead, I let him unzip his pants and watch them fall to the floor. His boxer briefs follow, and I drink in the glory that is Ethan Galloway.

My man.

My husband.

My future.

Resting my hands lightly on his hips, I look up at him and wobble out the words, "I love you so fucking much."

He grins, cupping my face and kissing me deeply. Wrapping his arm around my waist, he lifts me off the floor and walks us into the shower. The hot spray kisses our skin, and I groan at how good it feels. Every part of me aches, like my muscles have been carrying my stress and burdens for the last year and are finally starting to release the toxic energy I've been functioning on.

"Relax, baby," Ethan murmurs against my cheek. "I've got you."

His hands glide lightly down my arm, and he bends to

kiss the bruises. I tense, closing my eyes as the tip of his tongue caresses my tender skin, then start to relax when he reaches my shoulder, his gentle kisses trailing up my neck before finding my mouth again.

Sinking into him, I press our wet, naked bodies together and revel in the hard planes of his muscles. I love every curve and taut ridge.

His hard cock presses into my belly, but when I go to reach for it, he stops me.

"Let me wash you first."

Spinning me around, he faces me toward the shower spray, and I tip my head back, soaking in the heat, letting the warm steam wrap around me as he lathers up his hands and starts to wash off the grime I've been living with.

His hands are smooth and tender, gliding over me in a fluid motion. He massages my shoulders, working out the knots before trailing around to my front. His soapy fingers tease my nipples, and I groan, sinking against his torso.

I feel like he hasn't touched me in months.

My mind ticks, seeking out the memory of the last time we were together, and I can't even find it.

No, wait, it was...

Shit, we haven't been intimate since that angry sex we had on the couch back in... when even was that?

Weeks ago. Months, even.

It's a travesty.

Pressing my hand against the wet tiles, I steady myself

as he presses into me, his cock wedged against my back as his finger finds my aching clit and lightly massages it.

I moan, closing my eyes and panting as he works his magic.

He knows me so well. We've spent years discovering every crack and crevice of each other's bodies. We know our hot spots, what makes us quake and moan the loudest. He knows just how to make me writhe and whimper with pleasure.

"You're so sexy, baby." Brushing my wet hair aside, he kisses the back of my neck. I thrust my hips back into him, grinding our bodies together as my blood starts to boil with desire.

I'm so hot for him.

I'm probably dripping wet too.

In fact, I know I am.

I'm so ready for him to plunge into me, but he's making no moves to do that. Right now, his sole focus is pleasuring me, and I'm going to let him. Because this feels too fucking good to stop.

Leaning forward, I brace myself against the shower, the hot spray soaking my head, swallowing my cries when he pushes his fingers into me from behind. With one hand working my clit and the other thrusting into me, I'm undone within minutes.

I crack apart, splintering through the middle and crying against the shower wall. My entire body is buzzing with an electric current I'm not sure I can handle.

"That's it, baby." Ethan wraps his arm around my

waist, holding me up when my knees buckle, his fingers still inside me, working me until I am nothing but a limp mess, too weak to do anything but fall back against him.

The shower clunks off, and he lifts me off my feet, sweeping his arms beneath my legs and carrying me to the bed.

He leaves a trail of wet footprints in his wake, but he's too busy embedding his tongue in my mouth to notice. I drink him in, gripping the back of his neck and silently begging him to never let me go.

He places me on the bed like I'm a delicate petal, and I gaze up into his eyes. He's never treated me so gently before, but right now I'm tissue paper on the verge of disintegrating, and he somehow knows it.

Kneeling before me, he parts my legs, his eyes rich with affection as he crawls between them. His fingers are soft in my hair, brushing strands off my face as he hovers over me. He's silently asking for permission, the way he always does, and I softly smile, giving it the way I always do.

With a soft grunt he slips into me. It's a slow, languid movement, yet I still catch my breath. He fills me, wonder and ecstasy splashing through me as he stretches my core, filling my soul with warmth and my body with passion.

His eyes are still locked on mine, and I drink in his gaze as he moves within me. I match his rhythm, this slow dance of ours holding more meaning than it ever has before. Emotion clogs my throat, burning my eyes, and he stops, resting his hand on the bed and checking on me.

"Baby, what?"

"I just love you so much." I sniff, blinking at my damn stupid tears. "Shit, I never want to lose you, and I nearly did, and—"

"You'll never lose me," he cuts me off. "I promised to love and cherish you until the day I die." He moves inside me again, a slow thrust that takes my breath away. "You're mine and I'm yours forever, lil' mouse. You've gotta believe that."

"I do." I brush my fingers down his cheek, then tip my head back with a groan when he plunges deeper.

He kisses my chin, laughter bubbling in his throat. "I love you," he whispers, then plunges again. "I love you so fucking much."

His pace picks up, his thrusts coming harder and faster. I lose the ability to speak. All I can do is feel him inside me, taking over every sense and breath. Owning every one of my heartbeats.

"Look at me, baby."

My eyes pop open at his soft command.

Drinking in his gaze, I can feel his love all the way to my soul, then smile as his eyes start to glaze over.

"Oh fuck," he groans, his ass clenching as he drives into me.

I can sense his orgasm building and start to pant in time with him. His hand scoops beneath my ass, pulling me even closer as his thrusts take on an uncontrolled jerking quality.

His eyes snap shut, but I coax them back open.

"I want to look into your eyes when you come. Let me look at you, baby."

As soon as his gaze hits mine, I start to smile. Then his mouth pops open, another grunt firing out of him as he thrusts deep and hard. We stay connected as he finally lets go, releasing inside me with a musical groan that warms my heart. Our wet, slippery bodies press together, and I hold him tight as he tucks his chin into the crook of my neck and rides out the last of his high.

Wrapping my legs around him, I dig my heels into his ass and hold him inside me. Aware that he's squashing the breath out of me, he rolls us over. Our bed is wet, but I don't care. I continue to lie on his chest, clinging to him because I can't let go.

I have no idea how long we stay like that, but we just hang on like we're making up for lost time. Like we need to hold each other and soak in this bliss because life is fragile, and we've wasted too much of it being at odds with each other.

"I'm sorry I didn't listen to you sooner. I'm sorry I let that shitty job own me for way too long," I whisper.

"Hey." He nudges my chin up, so I perch my arms on his chest and start drawing patterns across his collarbone. "I should have been there for you. Been a better husband. And I'm sorry that I spent too long yelling at you and not enough time trying to support you."

My expression crumples, and he swipes his thumb beneath my eyes, but there aren't any tears to catch right now.

"It's over, Mick. It's done. We're gonna move forward from here."

"Yeah." My voice shakes and I nod. I've obviously still got more processing to do. I'm still feeling so weak and vulnerable. I really hate it.

"I feel like I've lost myself somehow." I frown. "Do you think I'll ever get me back?"

"You're still in there." Ethan cups my cheek, resting his thumb on the end of my chin. "And whether you believe it or not, right this second, you're a stronger version than you were before."

My laughter is a soft scoff. "I so don't feel like that right now."

"Yeah, I know. But you will." His eyes are so beautiful, and I drink in his gaze when he smiles. "We're gonna be stronger too."

"Yeah." I nod, my smile growing to match his.

"I'm with you every step of the way. Whatever you decide to do."

"Ditto." I sniff. "I know I'm not quite ready to start up my own agency yet, but that's the long-term goal, you know? I just need to find a different way of getting there."

"You could always contact some of your favorite agents and ask their advice. And if you need to move to have one of them as your mentor, I'll move with you, baby. It can't just be about my career."

I perch my chin on my hands and grin at him. "Wow. You really do love me."

"I adore you. And I know I don't always have a say on who I'll play for, and I have binding contracts I have to stick to, but never forget that you're more important to me than anything. If I have to move for you, I will. I'd find a way so that we can always be together."

I swallow, the sweet sentiment making me smile. "Ditto."

He kisses me again, then rolls me over when I start to shiver. Wrapping his arms around me, he tucks me against his side, then grabs the throw blanket off the bottom of the bed. We snuggle beneath it, and I finally drift off to sleep, wrapped in Ethan's arms and feeling at peace for the first time in months.

CHAPTER 29
CAROLINE

I have no idea what wakes me, but my eyes pop open and I gaze into the dimly lit room, immediately wondering where Casey is. Reaching for my phone on the nightstand, I check my texts and smile at the sweet message from my mom. It's a picture of Billy and Troy, blissfully snuggled up in the same bed together. They're sound asleep, their little mouths hanging open, Billy's reckless curls and Troy's sweet cherub face making my heart squeeze with affection.

I send a quick text back, filled with love-heart emojis, and Mom replies with the same. I smile at the screen, so incredibly grateful to have such wonderful parents. They have been serious lifesavers over the past few years, and I love how much they adore my children.

My mind instantly goes to my sweet girl, so tiny and vulnerable. I cried when Casey led me away from the NICU and made me get back into bed. I wanted to stay with her. It didn't matter that I could barely keep my eyes open. It didn't matter that my body was still aching and tender from pushing her out of me. I'm her mother, and she needed me.

Casey's soft coo and sweet words calmed me down, and he tucked me into bed, kissing my lips and promising me that our Lyla was in safe hands. I'd get to hold her again after another session in the incubator. At least she was strong enough that I was allowed to breastfeed her. My swollen, aching boobs are warning me that the time is coming up again soon. The nurse promised to come get me when little Lyla was ready for a feed.

I wonder where Casey is.

Slipping out of the hospital bed, I pad across the floor and grab his big hoodie, which he left over the back of the chair. It engulfs me, and I wrap the soft fabric around myself. I love the way it smells of his cologne and musky scent. He still turns me on with only a whiff, still makes me smile with just one look, and can still make my heart melt at the drop of a hat.

I never thought it was possible to score a guy like Casey Pierce. I never thought I would be with someone who gets me so hot and drives me so crazy. Someone who can infuriate me and then make me laugh all in the same heartbeat. Someone who I pine for when he's away and want to kick out of the house when he forgets to take out the trash or clean up the huge mess he and the boys made when they were playing. The house is always messier when he's home, but it's so bright and filled with energy when he's around too.

I love him.

I can't help myself.

I'll adore him for the rest of my life.

And I pine for him now, which is why I'm padding down the hospital corridor in my socks.

I pause at the nurses' station, but no one is there. Glancing around, I continue my quest, slowly working my way down to the NICU before finally spotting him.

And there goes my heart, melting into a big puddle of goo.

He's sitting in one of the nursing chairs, Lyla carefully tucked into his strong, tattooed arm. She's so tiny, it makes my heart squeeze. Casey has her wrapped up in a bundle so her little arms won't be jerking around and getting cold. Adjusting the hat on her head, he keeps talking to her, and the closer I get, the more his gentle hum turns into words I can hear.

"My precious girl. You are the most beautiful thing I've ever seen. And I'm going to look after you and make you laugh and teach you how to be strong and capable just like your mama." He lightly kisses the tip of her nose. "You're gonna have so much fun living in our house. Billy and Troy are a blast, and I'll show you all the best moves so you can stand up for yourself when they get too rough. They won't mean to, they're just boys. But I'm not gonna let them hurt you, okay?" Tipping his head, he studies her face, completely besotted with her. "And speaking of boys, you're not allowed to date until you're at least twenty-five, maybe even thirty."

I cover my mouth to stifle the giggle that's rumbling in my stomach. He sounds completely serious, and I love him for it. His voice is so tender, it soothes me all the way to my soul, and my eyes get misty as I watch them together.

"And my little Lyla, if you're ever in trouble, I'm the first guy you call, got it? I'm papa bear, and I'll keep you safe no matter what."

She makes a little noise, almost like a cry but not quite. She's getting hungry, I can sense it, but she settles when Casey starts talking again.

"So, you know, it'd be really awesome if you could be a daddy's girl. I know your mom is like the best human being on the planet, and if she becomes your favorite, I seriously will not hold it against you. But I've wanted a daughter since the first time she got pregnant. I've never told anyone this, but that first time, when we were still in college... I didn't think I could do the dad thing. I wasn't sure I'd be good enough, but then sometimes I'd let myself imagine, you know? And I'd picture a little girl with red curls and big blue eyes, and all I wanted to do was hold her and make her giggle and look after her." A vulnerable smile lifts the edges of his mouth. "And now I've got you. And that makes me so happy, lil' one." He sniffs like he might be fighting tears. "So, you stay strong for us, okay, sweet girl? And I'll be the best daddy in the world."

"Fact," I whisper, stepping into his line of sight. "You already are the best daddy in the world."

He grins at me, the boyish charm he exudes stealing my heart all over again.

He opens his arm to me, and I shuffle toward him, perching on the side of his lap and staring down at our beautiful daughter.

"She's perfect," I whisper.

"I know."

"How long have you been here?"

"Only fifteen minutes or so. The nurse said I could hold her until feeding time."

"She seems happy in your arms." I rest my cheek against his head. "I get it. Your arms are the best."

He squeezes my hip and looks up at me. I press my lips to his, loving this man more than I ever thought I could. He is everything I ever wanted and needed.

Easing away from him, I gaze back down at Lyla, my eyes glassing over when I say, "I'm sorry."

"What do you mean?" Casey gives me a questioning frown.

"For ever complaining about being pregnant again." I wince. "I'm sorry I yelled at you about that."

"Hey, it's okay. You were freaking out."

"I just didn't think I could do it." She shakes her head. "I feel so out of my depth sometimes, you know? Being a mom is hard."

"I know."

"But it's also wonderful. I love my kids so much." My

voice starts to shake. "They are so precious to me. And now we have this beautiful girl, and I *am* so grateful."

"Baby, don't cry," Casey whispers, squeezing me against his side and reaching up to kiss my cheek. "It's okay."

I sniff. "Blame it on hormones."

"'Kay. Will do."

We grin at each other, and he reaches forward again. I dip my head to kiss his lips, brushing my fingers through his hair.

Lyla starts to squirm, a pitiful baby cry coming out of her. I pull back, gazing down at our daughter and carefully taking her in my arms. Casey moves so I can have the chair, and the nurse comes over to check that everything is fine while I get settled breastfeeding. As soon as Lyla latches on, I take her little fingers. So tiny. They wrap around my thumb, and I'm overwhelmed with love for this precious little human in my arms.

"She's so tiny." My voice catches.

"I know, right?" Casey crouches down in front of me, lightly cupping her head. "When they put her in my arms before, I was freaking out that I'd break her or something. Billy was huge when he finally popped out, and even though Troy was smaller, he grew fast, you know?"

"That's because he needed feeding every twenty minutes." I give him a wry look.

Casey softly chuckles, then shakes his head. "Can you imagine what he's going to be like as a teenager?"

I let out a mock groan, then softly laugh, picturing my

boys as strapping teens and hoping they turn out as kind-hearted as their father.

"I get why you were scared when you found out you were pregnant again." His voice turns serious, his face filled with sweet compassion as he looks up at me. "But you are seriously the best mom. You're kind and fun and loving. I know the boys drive you crazy sometimes, but you're so good with them. You have the patience of a saint, and I wouldn't want to do this parenting thing with anybody else." His lips twitch. "Sometimes I feel like I should apologize that I keep accidentally impregnating you."

I snort and shake my head. It's not just his fault. We're too spontaneous and reckless sometimes. Lyla was conceived through a heated moment of passion, and while there may have been a condom involved, it was probably shoved on haphazardly in our rush to get on with it.

"The truth is, though... I'm not sorry. I love having babies with you. I love making them. I love watching your body change and grow this little human. And I love seeing our family get bigger. I love how chaotic and fun and crazy our house is. Getting home to you guys is the highlight of every day, and whenever I'm away, I miss you like crazy. I can't wait for everyone to be old enough so you can travel with me more. I love our family, Caroline. I love being a parent with you." His face is so sincere, his gaze so sweet.

I brush my hand down his cheek, the pads of my

fingers playing with his whiskers as I finally admit, "I love being a parent with you too. Even when it's hard, I wouldn't change it."

Lyla makes a sweet little guzzling noise, her arm flailing against my chest. I lightly take her hand again, kissing her soft, sweet skin and watching her feed.

I'm so blessed that it makes my heart hurt, and for some reason, my thoughts fly to Rachel. Sweet Ray, who was so kind to me as we rushed to the hospital. All the animosity was set aside as she made sure I was okay.

Sweet Ray who would be such an amazing mother but can't have kids.

My heart aches for her, and I want to call her, let her know how much I love and appreciate her. Apologize for leaving things after her outburst. I should have called her a few days later to check in, find out if she was okay, but I ghosted her.

She didn't yell at me that day because of something I did. She was hurting, and I've been a shitty friend. I let this bitterness between us grow, and I'm better than that.

As soon as the new day dawns, I'm calling her. We have to mend what's broken between us. And I have to find out the best way to move forward with our current situation.

Closing my eyes, I start quietly praying that there's a woman out there who needs a mother for her child, because I know Rachel would be freaking amazing.

CHAPTER 30
RACHEL

I thread my fingers together, then unthread them, smoothing out my floral pattern dress, then crossing my legs before unfolding them again.

Liam glances at me, softly laughing to himself as I continue to fidget. His large hand lands on mine, giving them a light squeeze.

"It's going to be okay," he reminds me yet again.

"What if they don't like me?"

"That's impossible." Liam shakes his head. "You're the most likable person I know."

I wrinkle my nose at him. "You have to say that. You're my husband."

"I'm your husband because I believe it. You think I'd marry someone I didn't like?"

A soft snort pops out of me and I shake my head, gazing out the window as we drive through town. The social worker called this morning to let us know that we'd been approved to foster these two children. We were allowed to come and collect them as soon as we were able. We took one long look at each other, then dropped everything, rushing to gather our things and get out the door.

As soon as Liam told me the idea of fostering these two children, my mind went into nesting mode. I spent the entire day on Sunday shopping and gathering supplies. The pool house is set up for two young kids, and I spent a near fortune making sure they had the best of everything. I got a new bed for each of them, toys and clothes. They'll probably come with their own stuff, but I lost my mind and suddenly had to prepare for every scenario.

Liam got home from work and blinked at the transformed pool house, then gave me one of his sweet smiles. "You know it's not definite, right?" He winced.

"I know." My head bobbed erratically. "And if they say no, I'll bawl my eyes out, then pack this stuff away, and it'll be good to go for the next time."

He picked his way across the room and pulled me into his arms. I rested my chin on his shoulder as his hands splayed across my back. "*Te amo, mujer hermosa.*"

I clung to him, then kissed his lips, and he carried me to our bedroom, where we lost ourselves in each other, drawing comfort from our lovemaking. It was just the distraction I needed as we waited for that phone call.

And then it finally came.

Now we're driving to a house where two no doubt

scared and traumatized children are waiting for Liam and me to take them into our home—to love them and help them heal.

My nerves are fried, frayed at the edges as fears and worries try to take me out. What if they hate living with us? What if we're not enough? What if they find a home in our place and are then sent back to El Salvador? What if their family changes their minds? What if—

"If you're playing the *What If?* game right now, please stop," Liam chides me. "That's only gonna send you into a tailspin."

I close my eyes and try to nod. "Yeah, I know. You're right. I just didn't sleep well last night, and my mind is..." I shake my head.

He squeezes my hands again. "Ray, we just have to take one day at a time, okay? We can't get too far ahead of ourselves. We need to love these kids in the moment and not think about the rest. Whatever comes, we can face it because we have each other."

I glance at him, my heart warmed by his sweet words. Raising his hand to my lips, I kiss the back of it before whispering, "Thank you. I love you."

"Love you, too, beautiful woman."

My smile grows a little wider, only faltering when my phone starts to ring and I notice the name on my screen.

"Who is it?"

"Caroline," I rasp.

He tips his head and pulls the car over.

"What are you doing?"

"You don't want this on your mind as well. Answer it. Deal with it. And then we can pick up these two kids with a clear head."

With a begrudging sigh, I slide my thumb across the screen and try to put on a bright voice. "Hey. How's it going?"

"Hey." Her voice is soft and tired.

"Everything okay with Lyla?"

"Yeah, she's in the incubator again. They're monitoring her breathing, and she's having sessions under those bili lights for her jaundice, but she seems strong. She can only handle small feeds, but they're frequent, and I'm holding her as much as possible."

My heart pinches, but I'm smiling as I picture Caroline with her new daughter. "I'm glad she's okay."

"Yeah, it's not the start I wanted for her, but I'm so incredibly grateful that she's going to make it through. Things are looking good at this stage."

"They'll stay that way," I assure her. "She's going to be just fine."

"Thanks." Caroline's voice starts to wobble. "Hey, Ray?"

"Yeah." I bite my lips together.

"I know things have been weird between us, and I just... I wanted to clear the air. I'm sorry if I hurt you when you came to visit that day. I can't remember what I said. I was stressed and tired and having the worst day. If I did anything to trigger you, I'm... I'm so sorry."

"No, it's—"

"Please, is it okay if I finish?"

"Yeah, of course." I wince, biting my bottom lip.

"And I'm sorry that I haven't called sooner. I just let it sit, you know? And I should have called to check on you. I knew how hard this all was for you, and I should have shown compassion and sympathy rather than backing off and hiding away from you. I really am sorry, Ray. You are the sweetest, kindest person I know, and I value your friendship so much. You—"

"Okay, it's my turn," I cut her off before the guilt can swallow me whole. "I... The way I behaved in your house was not okay. I was hurting, and I'd just found out the adoption had fallen through, and I didn't mean to lose it with you. I'm sorry. And I'm also sorry that I left things hanging. I should have called to apologize, but I didn't have the guts, and then for a second there I thought you were going to lose your baby or something, and I was heartbroken for you. It made me realize how much I love you as a person and as a friend, and I should have called you sooner."

Caroline lets out a watery laugh. "I love you too."

Tears smart my eyes, and I blink to stop them falling. "So, we're good, then?"

"Yeah, we're good." She sucks in a shaky breath. "I don't suppose you have time to swing past the hospital so I can give you a big ol' hug, do you?"

"I would, but..." I look to Liam and drink in his warm gaze. We share a smile, and he nods, so I tell her. "But right now we're on our way to pick up two foster children. They need a home, and—"

"Oh my gosh, that's amazing!" Caroline's voice pitches. "You will be the sweetest, kindest foster mother out there. I'm so happy you're doing this."

"Thanks." I brush a hand across my eye, catching the tears before they can fall. "I'm really nervous. I'm going from no kids to two, and I'm not sure if I'm cut out for it."

"You totally are. You are an amazing woman with a mother's heart. Those kids are so lucky to have you and Liam."

"I hope so."

"I know so." I can hear the smile in Caroline's voice, but then it drops to a serious lilt. "And I know you're probably scared that you're going to fall in love with them and they might get taken away from you, but Ray... you gotta have faith."

I nod, unable to speak past the lump in my throat.

"Now, tell me everything you know about these cherubs. What are their names? How old are they? What's the situation?"

A soft laugh punches out of me, and I quickly give her the rundown on three-year-old Carlos and his baby sister, Lucia, who has just turned seven months. I don't know much, but by the time I end the call, I am beyond ready to meet these kids.

"We're going to get to be mamas together. It makes me want to move back to Nolan just so we can have regular playdates!" Caroline exclaims.

I laugh along with her and am smiling by the time we hang up. I promised to come visit her at the hospital once our new kids are settled, and I'm actually excited to do it.

Liam starts the car, and the nerves kick in all over again.

Five minutes later, we're pulling up to the house, and I'm pretty sure I've stopped breathing.

"This is it, cariño. Time for you to meet our new foster kids."

"Okay," I whisper, my head bobbing erratically as I step out of the car and take Liam's hand. We walk up the sidewalk together, and I fidget with the buckle of my handbag while we wait for the social worker to answer the door.

"Hello there." She greets us with a bright smile. "Come on in. I'm so glad you were able to come today. I don't usually have kids stay with me, but our temporary foster family is already full, and I've been scrambling to find a placement for these kids. You two are a godsend."

I barely register what she's saying, my ears straining to hear sounds of small children. The second I detect a soft baby coo, my heart is catapulted right into that room. I round the corner, and there they are.

The boy is sitting on the floor, protectively hovering near his sister, who's propped up in a U-shaped pillow. She's obviously just learning to sit, and I kneel down with a smile as I watch her little arms flap about while she sucks on a plastic rattle.

"Hello," I say softly, capturing the boy's attention.

His head jerks up, and he stares at me with wide eyes. The toy train in his hand freezes midair as he takes me in.

Liam crouches down behind me and waves. "Hola, Carlos."

The boy studies him with a silent stare, his big brown eyes so young and vulnerable. He obviously recognizes Liam but is trying to figure out if it's safe to relax around him.

Liam's smile is kind, and he gently starts talking to the boy in Spanish. This seems to relax Carlos, and when he asks to see Carlos's train, the boy holds it out for him, a smile twitching the edges of his mouth.

Liam takes the train and starts making exaggerated choo-choo noises, driving the engine around in circles. Carlos smiles and shifts position, angling his body toward Liam. My gaze shifts to little Lucia, who's gazing at me with these pale brown eyes that make my heart squeeze.

"Hola, little one." I hold out my hand and she grabs my finger, pulling it toward her mouth and slobbering all over the end of it.

I laugh, and her chubby cheeks bloom with a smile.

My heart bursts with instant affection.

Carlos spins to check on her and gives me a cautious look before crawling back toward her, resting his little hand on her shoulder in a protective gesture that tugs on all my heartstrings.

"It's okay," I tell him, then switch to Spanish. Compared to Liam, my Spanish is stilted and slow. I've been learning ever since Liam and I started dating, and I've gotten so much better. I'm basically fluent, but I still can't speak as quickly as my husband.

The boy watches me as I talk to him, his nose wrinkling, then his little teeth starting to show when I tell him what a good older brother he obviously is.

"Such a big boy, taking care of your little sister," I tell him in Spanish. "She is so lucky to have you."

He gazes down at Lucia, leaning over to give her a kiss on the head. She topples sideways and the pillow catches her, but I reach out and steady her with my hand.

"Do you think you'd like to come back to our place?" Liam asks. "Rachel and I would love to look after you guys. We have a great house with a big yard. Rachel bought a bunch of toys yesterday, including a train set." He points at Carlos's train. "And we'd love to have you come stay. We can look after you guys."

Carlos looks past Liam's shoulder to the social worker standing behind us.

"That's right, Carlos." She bends down with a kind smile. "These are the people I was telling you about."

He looks back to us, his gaze darting between the two of us before finally nodding.

I give him a relieved smile, then ask, "Is it okay if I pick up Lucia?"

He nods again, and I reach for his little sister. The girl comes to me willingly, and I laugh as she bounces against me, her little legs flailing. I kiss her soft cheek and breathe in her baby scent, my heart overflowing when I picture walking into our house with these two. They are going to fill it with so much energy and life and love.

Even if we don't get them forever, we have them for now, and I am going to love them like they're my own.

It won't be hard. I can feel it in my very soul.

These two are meant to be with us.

And Caroline's right... I need to have some faith.

Liam and I are childless. Carlos and Lucia need parents.

It's meant to be.

Liam stands, bringing Carlos with him. His smile is rich with joy and excitement, and I can't help matching it.

"Shall we take these two home?"

"Yes." I grin, giving him a quick kiss before heading out to the car with a happy cherub in my arms.

CHAPTER 31
LANI

Thanks to not prebooking anything and then having flight delays, Asher's surprise took a lot longer to come to fruition than he expected. We arrived in Vegas at like three in the morning, and he was frazzled and frustrated by the time we finally booked a hotel room.

As soon as I saw the Vegas lights out the plane window, I knew his plan, and I was so there for it.

But not at three o'clock in the morning.

Once we checked into the hotel, I drew us a bath, massaged his tense body, and then made love to him, the water splashing out of the tub as I sat on his perfect cock and rode him until he was crying out my name and exploding inside me.

Now I'm walking down the Strip, the hot summer sun trying to melt my skin off as we prepare for our spontaneous wedding. Asher's already bought me a dress that is to die for—fitted white silk covered in sparkles and draping to the floor. I told him a Vegas wedding didn't need a fancy dress, but he wouldn't have it any other way, and I wasn't about to pass up the gorgeous gown. I'm sure I'll find an excuse to wear it again sometime, right?

All I need to do now is shower this sweat off my body, redo my makeup, and slide into the limo Asher has ordered for us.

My something blue is my sapphire engagement ring.

My something new is the dress.

And now I just need to find something old and something borrowed. I stupidly stress about it as I'm doing my makeup, and Asher must notice my tension as he's zipping up the gown.

"What is it, boo?" He gazes at my reflection, his eyes warm with appreciation as he runs his hands lightly over my hips. "You still want to do this, right? Because damn, woman, you look *so* fine."

I can't help a soft laugh. "Of course I want to." I spin, tweaking his bow tie, then wincing. "I'm being stupid."

"What do you mean?"

Against my will, my lips form a little pout, and I tell him, "I don't have something old or borrowed. And I know it's dumb to want the old, new, borrowed, blue thing, but... I'm only planning on getting married once, so..."

His smile gets all soft and mushy as he gazes down at me, then lightly pecks my nose. "We'll find something."

I look around the hotel room and raise my arms out

wide. "What? I'm not about to shove a hotel toothbrush down my bra."

He snickers and shakes his head. "First of all, no one *borrows* a toothbrush, and second..." He looks around, patting his pockets while he thinks, then stops and stares down at his hand.

"What?" I try to decipher the smile on this face.

With a little wiggle, he slips off his signet ring. Holding it between his thumb and forefinger, he grins at me. "My father gave this to me when I turned eighteen, just like his father gave it to him... and when my youngest son turns eighteen, I'm supposed to do the same." He takes my hand, and my fingers start to tremble at the idea of watching Asher's eventual son grow into a young man, knowing that the boy will be my son too. It makes my eyes burn as he slips the ring onto my middle finger. "I don't wear it that often because the guys always hassle me about being a rich prick, and the whole signet ring thing doesn't help. But for some reason, I slipped it on yesterday..." He raises my hand to his lips and kisses my knuckles. "And now I know why."

His wink turns my insides to putty, and if I hadn't just applied my lipstick perfectly, I would pull him in for a panty-melting kiss.

But that part can come later.

Right now...

"Let's go get married."

"As you wish, my love." He pulls me out the door, and we head through the hotel lobby and casino.

We get cheers and congratulations as we pass happy strangers.

For a second, I feel bad that none of my family and friends are here to see this, but there's also something super special about just being with Asher—my person. He's the one I was always meant to be with. It just took us a minute to figure it out.

Resting my head on his shoulder, I play with the buttons on the cuff of his tux until we pull up to the Amore Chapel. It's small and quaint and obviously new, although it's built like a chapel from the eighteenth century—white wooden panels with a pale blue trim.

I grin up at the steeple and thread my fingers between Asher's.

He looks like a giddy schoolboy as he bounces on his toes by the reception desk and gives the woman our names.

She's already got the paperwork waiting for us, and we walk down the aisle hand in hand. No big pomp and ceremony, just the way I wanted it.

The man who marries us is sweet and gentle, his voice quiet, and the lady who checked us in can't stop smiling as she bears witness to our nuptials.

Our vows are simple—the standard "I take you to have and to hold."

Asher's face as he says them to me is radiant, and I hope I shine just as brightly as I promise to stay with him for better or worse, for richer, for poorer.

My voice trembles when I say, "I do."

And his eyes are glistening when the minister pronounces us husband and wife.

There's no big applause or cheering as he pulls me into his arms. It's a quiet, intimate kiss filled with promise and belief.

"I love you," he murmurs against my mouth, and I cling a little tighter, deepening the kiss once more... until the minister clears his throat.

"We have another wedding in fifteen minutes. You might want to..." He rolls his finger in the air, and I start to laugh, then kiss Asher once more before taking his hand and practically skipping down the aisle.

The receptionist greets us, throwing confetti in the air as we walk through the foyer.

I spit the white circles out of my mouth, giggling as Asher does the same. We complete the paperwork, making everything official, and I sign my name below Asher's, a thrill whistling through me.

We're married!

Once outside in the sunshine, Asher pulls me into his arms again, and I melt against him.

"I love you, Mr. Bensen."

"I love you, Mrs. Iona."

I pull back before he can kiss me, playing with the ends of his hair. "Actually, I think I want to be Mrs. Bensen."

"Really?" His eyebrows rise in shock. "I for sure thought you'd want to keep your own name."

"Well, I do... for study, like my PhD and stuff, but... I

also really love the sound of saying, 'Hi, I'm Mrs. Lani Bensen.'" I can feel my cheeks flush as I bite my lips together. "What is wrong with me?"

Asher laughs. "You're pretty loved up right now, so I won't hold it against you if you change your mind later." He winks. "I don't care what you call yourself, just as long as you're mine."

"I'm yours." I wrap my arms back around him, loving the way his hands feel as they glide around my back and he secures me against him.

We stay in that mind-melting sunshine, kissing by the limo, until another bride and groom arrive with a little party of friends. With joyful congratulations, we wish them well, then slip into the limo and make out some more.

I hate to think what my makeup looks like between Asher's hot lips and the sweat melting my mascara off, but I'm too happy to care... until he gets a phone call from Liam.

"Hey. What's up?" Asher's eyes dart to mine, and I mouth, "Put it on speaker."

What? So I'm nosy.

He presses the speaker button, and I catch the end of Liam's question. "So, the kids are getting settled, and I wanted to let you guys know. You know, in case you're looking out the villa window and wondering why there's an adorable three-year-old running around in the yard."

I gasp. "You've got a three-year-old?"

"Oh, hey, Lani." Liam chuckles. "Yeah, it was all very

last minute, but we've got two foster kids until further notice."

"That's amazing," I gush. "I can't wait to meet them."

"Well, come on down if you like."

"Actually..." Asher clears his throat, and we share another look. "We're not home right now."

"Well, when you get back, swing by."

"We're in Vegas," my husband (Eeeppp! My husband!) admits.

There's a pause, and I can picture Liam's face as he slowly calculates that news and probably starts to draw some pretty accurate conclusions.

"Vegas."

"Uh-huh."

"What are you guys doing in Vegas?" I catch the smile in his voice, then hear Rachel.

"Vegas? They're in Vegas?"

I can't help a giggle and want to roll my eyes at myself. I sound like a schoolgirl.

Then Rachel's voice is coming through the speakers. "You guys didn't go to Vegas to get—" She gasps. "You totally did!"

I wrinkle my nose, my gaze completely goofy as Asher and I admit in unison, "We did!"

"Ah!" Rachel yelps, then orders us to stay on the line while she gets everyone else to dial in.

A few minutes later, we're listening to a bunch of overenthusiastic voices as they all try to figure out what's going on and what Rachel is babbling about.

"Okay, everyone, shut up!" Ethan calls through the speaker.

We all go quiet, and I hear him sigh while Mikayla stifles a giggle.

"That includes you, lil' mouse. We need to get to the bottom of this." His voice is playful and cute, like the Ethan we haven't seen in a while. Asher and I share a hopeful look.

"Have they made up?" I mouth.

Then Asher just gets to it and asks, "Hey, have you and Mick worked out your shit?"

Casey snorts and starts to laugh. "Always to the point, Bensen. Nice."

"You have no class," I whisper, my voice a teasing lilt.

He wiggles his eyebrows at me while Mikayla clears her throat and tells us, "Yes, marriage crisis averted. I don't want to go into it right now, but I can assure you that we will *both* be there for the Fourth of July picnic, and I will not have my phone with me."

Caroline and Rachel both cheer, and I blink back happy tears, relief pumping through me.

"Well, thank fuck for that," Casey mutters. "Now, why are we on this phone call?"

"Because Asher and Lani have some news to share," Rachel singsongs.

I blush and nearly call her out on *her* epic news, but this phone call has the potential of being way too long already, and we can catch up on all the latest goss at the July Fourth picnic.

"So, what is it?" Tammy asks.

I wince and quickly tell them, "We got engaged."

There's a collective gasp as I ease them into this.

"It happened just before the wedding, and we didn't want to steal anyone's thunder, so we kept it quiet," Asher explains.

"I knew something was up with you two," Casey murmurs.

"Yeah, they were sickeningly loved up at the rehearsal dinner," Ethan grumbles.

Asher grins. "Not apologizing for that. We had the best reason to be."

"So, you were engaged for less than a week?" Rachel balks.

"What!" Mikayla matches her tone. "What's that mean?"

"It means..." Asher looks at me again, his eyes so full of love they're practically shining. "We flew to Vegas to get married... and this sexy woman in front of me is now officially my wife."

The phone explodes with shocked surprise, and we let the voices drift around us as we lean together for yet another kiss.

The limo driver is patiently waiting as we stay in this chapel parking lot, making out and listening to our friends talking over one another as they process their surprise.

"You little shits." Mikayla's voice finally pulls us apart. "Sneaking off to get married without us. Damn, I wish I'd thought of that. We would have saved a fortune."

Ethan laughs. "You didn't love our wedding? Come on, babe. It was epic."

"It was epic, but Vegas sounds amazing!" Her voice picks up. "I'm so happy for you guys."

"Me too," Caroline pipes up. "And I can't wait to hear all the details when you get back. Lani, I mean *details*. Every tiny thing you can think of. I'm gonna want it all."

"I promise to deliver," I tell her, relieved she's forgiven me so easily for not including her. I was her maid of honor, and she has every right to be pissed at me for sneaking off without her.

"We're expecting to see you at our Fourth of July party, guys," Baxter says, finally joining the conversation. "No shirking off just because you're newlyweds."

I laugh. "We wouldn't miss it."

The annual event has become one of my favorite days of the year.

"Oh my gosh, can you believe it? The next time we get together as a group, we'll *all* be married." Rachel's voice is sweet with excitement. "Our Hockey House family has grown so much, and I'm just so grateful to each and every one of you. I love our family so much."

My eyes glass with tears because I can hear how much she means it. I can *feel* how much she means it, because I mean it too.

"I love you, guys," I tell them, emotion getting the better of me.

Asher brushes away my tears and leans in for another kiss. I'm not sure when everyone hangs up, but his lips and hands distract me all the way back to the hotel... and we spend the rest of our time in Vegas making love on every surface of that hotel room, eating delicious food from the various restaurants, and walking the bedazzled Strip at night.

By the time we get back to Nolan, I'm more loved up than I've ever been and ready to celebrate Independence Day with my favorite people.

THE HOCKEY HOUSE FAMILY:
<u>Back row:</u>
Rachel & Lucia, Liam & Carlos, Caroline & Lyla, Lani & Asher, Tammy & Baxter, Ethan, & Mikayla
<u>Front row:</u>
Casey, Troy & Billy, Nova, & Kai

You can check out a full-sized, color image of the Hockey House family on my website here:
www.katyarcher.com/the-hockey-house-family

This epilogue was so much fun to write, and every time I look at that photo, I feel my heart swell with love and affection for these characters. Which is why I'm so stoked that you'll still see some of them in the background of my next series—Nolan U Football.

It's time to head back to Nolan University and the Football Frat house. Timeline wise, the Hockey House bros will be in their senior year of college, and you'll be hanging with a bunch of sexy football players and the girls who win their hearts.

Find out more about my 2025 college football romance series here:
www.katyarcher.com/nolan-u-football

NOTE FROM KATY

Dear reader,

Writing this epilogue novella was so much fun. I love these characters so freaking much and to see five years into their future was a total treat.

At one point, I did wonder about holding off and releasing this later on... like literally five years down the track... but I just couldn't do it. I wanted you to see where these guys end up. I wanted you to feel all the joy I felt at watching them be established couples and dealing with the problems the next stage of life was throwing at them.

And you'll get to see it again... eventually... because I have plans for a 2nd generation series that will have you falling hard for Billy, Troy, Lyla, Nova, Kai, Carlos, Lucia...

and the kids who still haven't even been born yet. It's going to be so fun!

But for now, it's time to head back to Nolan U in the present day and enjoy falling in love with the guys all living in the Football Frat house. I've already started work on this series and I am buzzing! I can't wait to tell you more as the weeks roll by. Keep an eye on my Instagram and newsletter for updates.

If you enjoyed *The Forever Game*, I would so appreciate you leaving an honest review on Goodreads. Even just a star rating is helpful. You don't have to write anything if you don't want to. But star ratings and even short reviews really help validate the book, letting readers know it's worth a shot. It also tells book retailers that this novel is worth shining a spotlight on. I know there are a bunch of readers out there who love college sports romance just as much as we do. If you can help me reach them, then that would be freaking fantastic. Thanks for the assist!

I'd also like to thank a few key people who have helped me bring this epilogue novella together—Megan (the full-wrap cover for this one is my fave!), Kristin (for loving this story and making it as close to perfect as possible), Beth (for all the praise, encouragement and good ideas),

Rachael (for being such a great assistant). I love you guys 🤍

My review team—thanks for all your excitement over this one. Being able to give you this story has been the best!

My readers—you have made this my most epic year ever. Seriously. Your love for this Nolan U Hockey series has been a huge game changer for me and I cannot say thank you enough. I so appreciate and love you for inviting these characters into your world and wanting to hang out with them at Nolan U!

Trudi—you are amazing and kind and encouraging. I love our lunches, our brainstorming chats and the way you always make me feel so uplifted. Thank you.

My God—you put these stories into my heart and it's been nothing but a joy to write them. Thanks for your constant love and inspiration.

xoxo
Katy

BOOKS BY KATY ARCHER

NOLAN U HOCKEY
Hockey House V-cards (prequel)
The Forbidden Freshman
The Heart Stealer
The Game Changer
The Love Penalty
The Only Goal
The Forever Game

NOLAN U FOOTBALL
Releasing in 2025
The Forever Play
The Off-Limits Play
The Surprise Play
The Illicit Play
The Perfect Play

<u>NOLAN U BASKETBALL</u>

Releasing in 2026
In development

CONTACT KATY

I love to hear from my readers, so feel free to email me anytime. You can also find out more on my website.

EMAIL: katy@katyarcher.com

WEBSITE: www.katyarcher.com

And if you want to connect with me on social and see pretty reels and teasers from the books, you can find me Addicted to College Sports Romance on...

INSTAGRAM
@addictedtocollegesportsromance

FACEBOOK
@collegesportsromancebooks

TIKTOK

@katyarcherbooks